THE
JIGSAW MAN

THE
JIGSAW MAN

David Hunter

RUTLEDGE HILL PRESS
Nashville, Tennessee

Published in Nashville, Tennessee, by Rutledge Hill Press, Inc., 513 Third
Avenue South, Nashville, Tennessee 37210

Typography by Bailey Typography, Inc., Nashville, Tennessee

Library of Congress Cataloging-in-Publication Data

Hunter, David, 1947–
   The jigsaw man / David Hunter.
     p. cm.
   ISBN 1–55853–094–0
   I. Title.
PS3558.U46964J54 1991   90–21883
813[f.54-dc20   CIP

Printed in the United States of America
1 2 3 4 5 6 7 8 — 96 95 94 93 92 91

I dedicate this book to my fan of longest standing, my mother, Helen Goin Hunter.

Prologue

The old bridge creaked and moaned as the headlights of the vehicle opened a circle in the night. The green paint, peeling and ragged, had left spots of orange rust showing on the metal span. One day the county would get around to condemning it as unsafe. Few cars crossed it, though, since the new bridge a mile down the Holston River had been completed, so there had been few complaints about its condition.

The car stopped and the headlights died, leaving the area in darkness except for the light of a full moon which dimmed from time to time as clouds scuttled across its face. The only sound was of water lapping against the pilings below.

The door on the driver's side opened, sounding unnaturally loud in the dark silence, and a figure made its way to the rear of the car. There was a scratching sound as a key slid over the paint seeking the locking mechanism. Finally the two connected, and the trunk lid popped open as the key was turned.

Reaching inside, the driver grabbed a silver bag of the type used to line kitchen garbage cans. With a grunt the driver hoisted it out by the neck which was closed with a wire tie.

Alongside the railing, the dark figure swung the bag back and forth a couple of times, gaining enough momentum to clear the railing. The silver bag arched out, glimmering in the moonlight.

"Good-bye, head," the driver said with a satisfied chuckle, listening as the bag struck the water sixty feet below with a faint splash.

9

On the banks of the Holston, a hundred yards from where the bag had splashed down, a raccoon turned her masked face toward the sound, startled as she was gnawing open a small fresh-water mussel. Sensing no imminent danger, she went back to her meal.

She heard the car start and drive away. That, however, was the business of mankind and of no concern to the wild creatures of the night.

Chapter One

Doyle Griffin strolled into Chet's Place, leisurely looking around to see who was there. He was a tall man, with hair already silvery white at forty-two. His three-piece pin-stripe suit hung neatly from his lanky frame, even after nine hours of wear.

Chet's Place was not a cop bar. Doyle avoided bars that were popular with cops. When he was through for the day, the last thing he wanted was to discuss police work. Although he was fond of his brother officers, he wanted distance between himself and the job after hours.

Chet's Place was a small block building, garishly painted, with a sign in the window that said it was the "home" of a once-popular country singer by the name of Ray Flynn. What actually had happened was that the singer had gotten riproaring drunk there once in the days before fame had come to him. Ray would have been surprised to see the sign.

In his three-piece suits, Doyle looked out of place in the little hole-in-the-wall bar. Its few regular patrons had gotten used to him and often boasted that a "famous homicide cop" drank with them. To them "famous" meant having one's name in the local papers from time to time.

"Everybody be careful," the chubby bartender said, "there's a cop in the house!"

Doyle smiled in acknowledgment. He had learned to accept such comments years earlier as part of the job.

11

In the back of the room, a bleached-blonde woman—a young forty or an old thirty—turned and stared at him curiously. The rest of the patrons were regulars, already used to Doyle and his three-piece suits.

"Give me a Michelob, Chet."

"Sure will, Officer," Barney, the bartender, said with a chuckle. This was an old joke between them. The founder of the bar had been dead fifteen years and Barney, the only bartender, had bought the place from Chet's widow. He had decided that changing the sign was not worth the expense.

"You workin' on a whodunit tonight, Doyle?" The bartender was a big man, going soft, with a scar running from his left eyebrow to his receding hairline. He set the Michelob on the bar.

"I got lots of whodunits, but I'm not workin' on any of 'em tonight. I'm gonna drink a couple of beers, then head home. First thing in the mornin', I'm gonna turn on my answerin' machine and go fishin'. I'm gonna fish for a week."

"Who's gonna fight crime while you're gone?"

"We gotta brand-new rookie homicide officer just rarin' to make a name for himself. I reckon by the time I get back, he'll have it all under control." Doyle turned up the beer and swallowed half of it.

"How many homicide officers you got?"

"Four, and a supervisor who helps out." Doyle finished the beer, and Barney put another one out.

"That seems like a lot," the bartender said. "Ain't like there's a murder every day."

"We work rapes and assaults, too."

"I guess there's a lot of them."

"Yeah," the officer said, tilting the bottle again, "and they cause the same amount of paperwork as murder."

"Hello, cutey-pie."

The bleary-eyed, bleached blonde was standing a foot from Doyle's shoulder. Up close, he revised his estimate of her age. She was well past forty.

"Howdy," the officer said politely.

12

"Wouldja buy a lady a beer?"

"Sure. Barney, set the lady up." Doyle stood and drained his beer. He took out a money clip and tossed a bill on the bar. "Keep the change, Barney, but don't spend it all in one place."

"Hey!" The blonde nearly fell off the stool. "Whassa matter? You too good to drink with me, or what?"

"Honey, I'd be delighted to drink with you," Doyle answered, flashing her a smile, "but I just had a vasectomy and I don't think I can stand the temptation."

"What'd he say?" the blonde asked as the door closed behind him.

Sammy Turpin sipped the horrible coffee from a paper cup marked with the logo of Hal's All Night Market and tried to make himself comfortable in the front seat of his unmarked car. Working criminal intelligence for the Horton County Sheriff's Department had always been a lonely job.

"Can you believe it?" Sammy would often rave to his long-suffering wife. "The department's got five friggin' German shepherds and ten motorcycles. But I have to work alone! They can't see that good intelligence *prevents* crime."

"I know, dear," his wife would always reply. "They just don't appreciate your importance. You should go back to patrol where you were appreciated."

Sammy would never voluntarily give up his job, though. His hatred for outlaw motorcycle riders in general and the Devil's Sons in particular kept him going. It was his ambition to put all of them in the penitentiary, where they belonged.

Picking up the binoculars, he looked again through the window of the house across the street, the local headquarters for the Devil's Sons. A party was in progress, and Sammy was keeping a log of the people in attendance. He knew most of them as well as his own family, having spent years staring at them through binoculars and telephoto lenses.

This had been a relatively sedate party, with the exception of a fight between a regular called Bonzo and a big, blond man that Sammy didn't know. The fight had spilled into the kitchen, so he didn't know who had triumphed. Bonzo had fought with almost everyone at one time or another.

It had been quiet for two hours. Not even the bare-breasted woman could hold his attention. He had nude photos of her in his files anyway. Biker women spend a lot of time naked, most of them being exhibitionists at heart.

Sammy was about to call it a night when the side door of the clubhouse opened. The outlaw bikers seldom used that door. A man emerged carrying what appeared to be a garbage bag, which he lugged to the street and hefted onto the back of a pickup truck. He was followed by two more men.

After carrying out several more bags, they all climbed into the old pickup and drove away. Watching closely as they pulled under a street lamp, Sammy identified them. All the male members from the party, except for the big blond guy who had been fighting with Bonzo, were in the truck.

Turpin watched the house closely for a few more minutes. The women seemed to be involved in an animated conversation. Briefly he wondered what had happened to the blond guy, then shrugged. *Probably passed out*, he decided as he noted the activity in his log and called it a night.

His wife would be packed and ready to go when he got home. They were driving down to Florida—Panama City— for a few days. He could file his report when they returned.

Chapter Two

Holbert's Quarry is one of many abandoned mining operations dotting the rugged hills of East Tennessee. It flourished in the days before protecting the environment became a powerful political issue. Operators would simply find an available source of limestone and keep digging as long as it was easy to reach. Then they would move on to a more readily available source, leaving the hillside raped and bare.

Underground springs would quickly fill the pits. Some of them, like Holbert's Quarry, were a hundred feet across and seventy-five feet deep.

Since no one was interested in useless holes in the ground, the quarries generally became illegal dumping grounds, inhabited by snakes, spiders, rats, and frequently used by lovers seeking a little cheap privacy.

At Holbert's Quarry, trash of every description was scattered around, everything from stacks of tires to old mattresses. The miniature lake had also become a watery repository for stolen cars, mostly insurance scams. A citizen who could not pay for his car would hire someone to steal it and dump it where it would not be found, not for a long time anyway.

Terry Mulligan and Dean Clowers had come to Holbert's Quarry to look for cars that morning. They were "salvage men," scavengers of car parts, which they refurbished and sold to junk yards. Using an old flatbed truck with an ancient cable hoist, they would fish around until they hooked onto something solid. It was not an efficient method, but it served their needs.

Terry Mulligan stood in the early morning light, waiting for his partner to back the truck to the edge of the quarry, savoring a cup of coffee amidst the trash, insects, and used condoms. It was unusually warm for a Tennessee October approaching November.

"Move that silver garbage bag," Dean Clowers yelled.

"Run over it," Terry replied mildly.

"At least see what's in it. I don't want to bust a tire," Clowers demanded irritably.

With a shrug, Terry walked over to the garbage bag, wrinkling his nose at the odor. *It smells like burnt meat,* he thought as he peered closer in the dim light. He could see that the bag was lying on several tires. Someone had tried to burn the pile of tires and the bag, and one side was scorched and melted.

Bending over, still sipping his coffee, Terry jerked on the plastic bag. As its contents spilled out, he poured coffee all over himself while recoiling from the object. Hurling the coffee cup down, he ran to the cab of the truck.

"Get to a phone, Dean. Quick!"

"What's wrong?"

"It's a body, or part of a body. Let's go!"

"You're crazy, boy." Dean ponderously lowered his 230 pounds to the ground and ambled back to the pile of garbage. At the smell of burnt flesh and the sight before him, he fought back a gag reflex.

Gary Keith propped his feet on the desk. It would have been a pleasurable day, except for the hangover. He had been up until two that morning celebrating his promotion to investigator. As usual, Neptune's Lounge had been full of officers who were happy to join his celebration.

The cops had started out toasting Gary's success. Afterwards they toasted the department, the county, the state, the flag, the armed forces, and Dolly Parton. They had then toasted all the letters of the alphabet. Gary had left on the letter G, but hardly anyone had noticed at that stage of the game.

He seldom drank heavily. When he was drunk, his perfect diction, perfected with a tape recorder, would begin to slip into the speech of his childhood, and he was careful to keep that childhood hidden from his fellow officers.

Appearances were important to Gary Keith. Raised in a federal housing project, he had been ragged and poor as a child. He had worked his way through the University of Tennessee with no outside help. Along the way he had learned to dress and speak well. Most of those who knew him assumed that he came from an upper-middle-class family, and he had never told them any differently.

He shuddered as the phone rang. To his sensitive ears, it was painfully loud.

"Homicide, Keith."

"This is dispatch. They need you at Holbert's Quarry. They have a human torso."

"Pardon?" Keith hoped he had heard wrong. A torso was not the proper kind of call with which to start a career in the homicide division.

"They've got a human torso at Holbert's Quarry. Patrol is already on the scene."

"All right, thanks." He hung up the phone and sat staring ahead for a moment. Keith was often called "an intellectual" by his coworkers, most of whom considered it abnormal to read books on psychology and sociology unless one was taking a test. He was a pale man of medium height, thirty years of age, with a high forehead and piercing black eyes. His face was rimmed by thin wire-framed glasses.

"Damn," he swore, picking up his radio and clipboard. He would have to bother the lieutenant his first morning on duty, but there was no way he was going to chance botching something this important.

Stopping at Howard Mull's office, he spoke. "Lieutenant.

I've got one that you'd better look at. A torso up at Holbert's Quarry."

"I know," his supervisor answered. "I was listening to the radio. I wondered if you'd have enough sense to call me before you went up there." Slipping on his blue blazer, he locked the door behind him, reflecting that the college boy might be smarter than he acted most of the time.

The patrol officer tiredly waved back a new clump of people who were trying to crowd in for a closer look.

Where have they all come from? she thought. It was only seven-thirty in the morning, and forty people already were crowded around the quarry. With relief, she saw the un-marked homicide unit bumping along the gravel road.

The door opened and Lieutenant Mull slowly got out. At fifty, he had been around a long time. There were few lines in his face, but a twitch in his left cheek was a reminder of the tension he had endured for twenty-five years. Normally his face twitched occasionally, maybe once an hour. Under stress, it showed up every few minutes. While he had learned to live with the problem, it made rookies nervous.

"What do we have, Ruth?" Mull tried to remember at least the first names of all patrol officers that he met, but he was not always successful. The department was growing. He had been the only homicide investigator at one time, many years before. The pretty, blonde officer was a relative newcomer.

"We have a human torso, male. The arms are missing at the shoulders, the legs about halfway up the thigh. Genitals are missing, and it looks like it's been gutted. Also, it appears someone tried to burn it, but the tires didn't catch on fire. Just scorched the flesh a little."

"Have you talked to the witnesses?"

"Yeah, the two over by the truck found it. The kid over there," she pointed with her chin, "the one with the red head-band, says he was here last night and thinks the bag was here then."

"Good work, Ruth." He admired the cool way she was handling herself. The scene was enough to shake an officer with more time than she had on the job. She was a sturdy woman in her late twenties, but not so sturdy that he failed to notice the feminine curves that showed through her uniform. Her pale blonde hair was pulled back in a no-nonsense bun.

"Call the coroner, Gary. I want him to take a look at this one before we move it. You don't have much to go on with a torso. No prints and no dental charts. Tattoos and scars are about your only hope."

Mull walked past the patrol officer and, fighting revulsion, leaned over for a closer look. *It never gets any easier,* he thought, *even after hundreds of bodies.* Man's capacity to inflict pain and suffering continued to amaze him.

"The coroner's on his way, Lieutenant," Gary Keith reported, staring at the torso in morbid fascination.

"Come closer, son. Let me point out some details."

Keith's first assignment as a homicide investigator had begun.

Shep Hankins slowly reeled in his line as the afternoon sun glinted off the water of the Holston River, turning it into a mirror. It had been a slow afternoon. The fish just did not seem interested.

Reaching for a pair of sunglasses from his wicker basket, he put them on. Pulling a red bandana out of the basket, he wiped his forehead. It was unseasonably warm. The jacket had felt good when he left the house that morning, but he would have to shed it now.

Shep stood and stretched, taking off the jacket. Retirement was not what he had hoped. In fact, it was downright boring. Fishing was not nearly as much fun when you could do it anytime you wanted. *It's a lot like sex,* he thought with a silent chuckle. *It's all you think about, until you can have all you want.*

Picking up his rod, Hankins made a long cast, then began to reel it in quickly. As the fly got within twenty feet of the bank, it passed over something half submerged in the water. It was silvery gray.

Casting back out, he tried to snag the object. On the third try, he succeeded and reeled it in slowly. "Whatever's in the bag sure is heavy," he muttered. Picking it up, he walked away from the edge of the river, then put the bag down. It was closed with a wire tie.

Catching the bag by the bottom, he dumped it on the sandy ground. It took Shep's eyes a moment to adjust to the object that rolled out. It was about the size of a large cantaloupe.

"My God!" He took a step backwards, almost falling down, then vomited.

A human face stared up at him. It seemed calm, not at all what one would expect of a head found in a garbage bag. Shoulder-length blond hair and a long, blond mustache framed the face.

The neck ended in a jagged line just below the chin.

"We appreciate it, Doctor."

Lieutenant Mull hung up the phone and turned to Gary Keith. His tic was jerking about every three minutes. They had just finished up at the scene where the torso had been found, when they were summoned to the banks of the Holston River to meet with a near-hysterical retired railroad engineer who had found a head in a silver garbage bag.

"Here's what the coroner's got so far. The head and the body match. The time of death was sometime in the last forty-eight hours. It's a white male, late twenties to early thirties, big fellow by the size of his chest, maybe two-twenty body weight. There was a puncture wound through his right eye, entering his brain, that was severe enough to have caused death. Possible weapon an ice pick or thin screwdriver. The victim suffered a severe head injury several years ago. Also, three .22 caliber rounds in his chest cavity. The doc says we'll find the entrails somewhere else. The body *was* gutted, just like the patrol officer said this morning."

"So what's the cause of death?" Keith asked.

"They say we won't know that until we find the killers. The bullets *or* the head wound could have caused death."

"The patrol officer told us most of that this morning."

"Findin' murderers ain't a science, son. People think it is, but it ain't. Catchin' murderers is an art."

"Well, I think we can at least expect to find the rest of the body parts in the east end of the county, say within a three mile radius," Keith said.

"Maybe, maybe not. First thing you need to do is get the dental charts from the coroner and have 'em run in the paper. Also, get an artist from one of the papers to do a sketch of the head. We can't solve the murder 'til we know who was murdered."

The phone rang and Keith picked it up. "Homicide, Keith." It seemed like more than eight hours since he had answered the phone the first time. He sat listening, his mouth tightening into a grim line.

"All right." He hung up the phone. "So much for my theory. They just found another set of parts. Two sets, as a matter of fact. One set in a silver garbage bag, the other in an old suitcase. They turned up in the north this time—at least twelve miles from the others."

"You go ahead, Gary. Just do a close crime scene search like the last two times. Make sure Criminalistics shoots plenty of good pictures. Let the coroner take everything with him."

"You're not going, Lieutenant?"

"No, I've got somethin' I have to do." He got up tiredly and put on his coat. "Detail, son, just pay attention to detail. That's how we catch 'em."

Howard Mull drove slowly toward his destination. He was tired. Never had he shirked his duty, but he was tired. The twitch in his face was worse than it had been in years. He had taken the supervisor's job because he had to, not because he wanted to sit behind a desk.

Pulling into the parking lot of an apartment complex, he looked for an old, blue Ford. It was not there, so he backed into an empty space and waited. It was not long before the car arrived. He watched as tall, lanky Doyle Griffin got out and opened his trunk, picked up a string of fish, and started toward his apartment. Howard Mull got out and followed him.

"Doyle."

The tall detective turned. A smile crossed his face.

"What brings you out, Lieutenant? As if I didn't know."

"You been listenin' to the news today?"

"Yeah, I heard it on the way to the lake this morning. Found any more parts yet?"

"The head, and some more that Keith's gone to look at now."

"I was really lookin' forward to bein' off this week, Lieutenant," the detective said, even before the question was asked. He opened the apartment door.

"I know, Doyle, but I need you bad. Keith's a good officer, for a college boy, but this one is gonna take street savvy. Will you do it?"

"You've forgot more than I'll ever know, Lieutenant. Why don't you handle it?"

"Fix me a drink, Doyle, bourbon if you have it, and I'll tell you a secret."

He sat quietly while Griffin fixed two bourbon and waters, walked back into the living room, and handed one to the lieutenant.

"Tell me a secret," Griffin said.

"You remember the Voiles case, Doyle?"

"Yeah, the last one you worked on before you took the supervisor's job. A fine piece of police work, Howard."

"That day when we went down to the lake and recovered the girl's body—there was a thirty-pound rock holding her head under—somethin' happened. She didn't look real bad, not as bad even as what we saw today, but somethin' happened inside me. I knew as we were takin' her out of the water that I'd worked my last homicide. I've seen too many. Look at me, Doyle. The twitch is so bad I can't concentrate. I went out there with Keith today, but I didn't want to be there.

"I'm retirin' soon, Doyle. I'd like to go out with dignity. I got nobody else to assign, not that can do it like you will. I'm askin' you as a favor, Doyle—a favor for a tired old cop."

"All right, Lieutenant. I'll be there first thing in the morning. I reckon the fish ain't goin' nowhere."

Chapter Three

The woman slowly turned the pages of the newspaper. Her lips moved as she followed the text with her finger, as she had been taught in public schools fifty years before. Her face was grim, attesting to a life that had never been easy. Her cheap wash-and-wear dress was faded, worn much longer than its manufacturer had intended.

The back door opened and her son came in. He was a burly man in his thirties with the same grim expression found on his mother's face, but his face showed more than determination. His piercing black eyes smoldered in rage. He shrugged the coat off his massive shoulders and hung it on a nail beside the kitchen door.

"Did you read about the cut-up body they been findin' pieces of?" she asked.

"I heard 'em talkin' about it at the feed store," he said, washing his grimy hands in the kitchen sink. "What's for supper?"

"Pinto beans with ham and turnip greens. It's warmin' on the stove. The torso wasn't too far from here—just down at Holbert's Quarry."

"Yeah, that's what I heard." He got down a plate and began to ladle out beans and turnip greens. "We got any onions?"

"There's a cup of 'em already sliced in the refrigerator. This chopped-up body sounds like the devil's work," she said.

"That's somethin' you oughta know about, Ma. You lived

with his first cousin for twenty-five years. The *Reverend* Cleveland Waters! Saver of souls!"

"Your father wasn't an evil man, John. He was raised hard and didn't know any other way." Her blue, watery eyes watched his face closely.

"You call it like you see it, Ma. I'll call it like *I* see it. A man that beats his son with a leather strap and locks him in a dark basement is more than a *little* hard. He was a sanctimonious, two-faced hypocrite. I don't want to hear anymore about it!" His eyes flashed as he glared at her.

"I need the clothes you was wearin' yesterday," she said, changing the subject. "I'm gonna do a wash."

"I threw 'em away," he mumbled, spooning in a mouthful of beans and turnip greens. "Got grease on 'em while I was workin' on the tractor."

"All right, son." He had thrown them away. That much was true. She had found them when she carried out the trash from the kitchen. There was no grease on them, though. They were covered with blood.

She watched her son as he chewed his food and read the newspaper. The silver glint of metal danced in the matted hair behind his open shirt collar each time his powerful jaws moved. The emblem sent chills up and down her spine. It was not a Christian symbol, not a cross. It was a pentagram, a five-pointed star, the symbol of Satan.

"I'll be down at my workshop," he said, pushing back the heavy wooden chair.

"I was hopin' you'd stay up here tonight, maybe watch some television."

"Nope. I got work that has to be done."

After he had left, she stood at the window and watched as he walked across the field. His workshop, as he called it, was a room attached to the barn, once used to store feed. After the death of his father, he had cleaned it out and moved things in. She never knew what was in there. He kept the door padlocked, and she was afraid to look.

How could a boy raised in a house where Jesus was King

25

stray so far? she wondered. He had not been inside a church since his father died, mangled in a hay-baling machine, with John as the only witness.

With a sigh, she tied up the garbage can liner and went to get a fresh one from under the sink. Taking out the box, she froze. Shivers ran up and down her spine again. Her eyes went from the newspaper to the box of silver garbage bag liners in her hand.

She always bought the black bags. John must have bought these since the last shopping day. The box was open and several bags were already gone.

Gary Keith looked up curiously as Doyle Griffin entered the office, sipping steaming coffee from a crockery mug with pigs on the side. Keith neither drank coffee nor smoked, which set him aside from most cops even more than the books he read.

"I thought you were on vacation, Sergeant." He took a sip of a diet soft drink that was on his desk.

"I been called off vacation," Doyle sighed, sliding into a worn and heavily padded chair. "The lieutenant's got too much other stuff to do. Says he can't do the case justice, so I'm gonna help you."

"You mean, I'm going to assist *you*."

"No, I mean just like I said. This is your case. I'll be assisting. You just got unlucky. Everybody gets one like this eventually. You just started early. Why don't you tell me what you have so far."

"All right," Keith began. "Body parts have been found in three places so far. The torso was at Holbert's Quarry. Arms cut off at the shoulder, legs in the middle of the thigh, and it was gutted. An attempt was made to burn it, but the fire didn't catch. The torso was in a silver garbage bag.

"The head was pulled out of the Holston River by a fisherman yesterday. The place where he found it is not accessible by car. I'm guessing it was tossed from the bridge, about three hundred yards upstream.

"The third bunch of parts was found behind a church at a place where illegal dumping goes on, in the north. Both legs, cut into three parts each, were in a silver garbage bag, like the other ones. There was also a brown suitcase, a very old suitcase. It contained intestines, the stomach, the entire scrotum, and flesh that appeared to have been carved off the thighs."

"What about the penis?"

"It wasn't there. Do you think that's significant?"

"I don't know. Maybe, maybe not. How about the heart and liver?"

"They haven't turned up yet."

"So we're still missin' the arms, the major organs, and the penis?" Griffin asked, stretching out his long legs across the small room Keith and he shared with two other investigators.

"That's correct," Keith answered. "It's like putting together a jigsaw puzzle."

"Don't say that in front of the press. They love catchy names. They're already callin' it the 'Torso Case.' Don't give 'em anything new."

"Have I told them too much?" Keith sounded alarmed.

"Don't panic, Gary. It's early yet. We'll hold back some, but we need to work with the press. Sometimes they're the only thing we have. What's the coroner say the cause of death was?"

"Either a sharp object into the brain, through the right eye, or the gunshot wounds. I figure the three shots were fired and the stab wound was the coup de grâce."

"When does the coroner pinpoint the time of death?"

"Within forty-eight hours is the best he can do. It was unseasonably warm yesterday, but the temperature got down below thirty the night before that."

"You've already given the dental chart to the papers and had their staff artists do a sketch of the head, right?"

"Right. The sketches and the charts will run today."

"Anything else at the scene?"

"There was a tag on the suitcase, but it was too faded to

read. The F.B.I. is going to try to bring it up, but it'll take a couple of days."

"What do you think, Gary? What's your gut feelin'?"

"I think it's a warning to someone, an act of retribution. The mob, or maybe even outlaw bikers."

"That's a possibility, but who was the message delivered to? If the head had turned up in a mailbox, I'd grab that theory. But . . . I just don't know."

"What do *you* think, Doyle?"

"Ritualistic, maybe. That's why I asked about the penis and the heart and liver. But it may not mean anything. We need to get ahold of Sammy Turpin. He knows more about outlaw bikers than anyone I know."

"I've already tried to call him. He won't be back until Thursday. He's gone to Florida. Also, I've got in a call for an anthropologist up in Massachusetts who specializes in ancient religions."

"Well, well," Griffin raised his eyebrows, "maybe you don't need me after all! Maybe I should just go back to fishin'."

"No, I'm sure I'll need your help—" He was interrupted by the telephone.

"Homicide, Keith." The investigator's brows drew together as he listened. "Thanks," he concluded.

"That was the receptionist. We've got a guy at the front desk who wants to confess to the torso killing. This case may not take as long as we thought."

"I reckon we'll see," Griffin answered. "I'll go down and get him."

"That's him over there," the receptionist spoke gently to Doyle Griffin. "He's *really* weird." The receptionist wore her hair in a "punk" cut, much like the "mohawk" popular with boys back in the fifties. Each pierced ear held three kinds of earrings, and her nails were striped green and yellow.

"Thanks. Would you come this way, sir."

"Certainly." The man was thin and nervous, his sandy hair receding halfway back. He walked in quick, mincing steps. A small man, about five-seven, maybe 135 pounds, he was wearing a gray suit of an obviously expensive cut, with highly shined loafers.

They walked without speaking down the long hall to the homicide office where Gary Keith had already set up the tape recorder and had a blank pad in front of him. He stood as they entered.

"I'm Investigator Keith, and you're . . . ?"

"My name is Quinton J. Calley." He extended a birdlike hand to Keith, looking over the investigator's shoulder at the map of Horton County, with colored pins showing where the body parts had been found.

"Would you like a cup of coffee or a soft drink, Mr. Calley, before we get started?"

"No. The caffeine makes me nervous."

"Have a seat, then, Mr. Calley. This is Sergeant Doyle Griffin. What was it you wanted to talk to us about?"

"Why the murder, of course. I told that to the atrocious looking young woman at the front desk. I can't imagine why an agency would hire a person who *insists* on looking like that." He crossed his legs primly.

"Fact is, she didn't look like that when they hired her," Doyle chuckled. "She changed completely after her probationary period. It's hard to fire a county employee without cause."

"Well, it looks to me like they could get rid of someone who dresses for Halloween at work."

"Mr. Calley," Keith cleared his throat, obviously impatient with the conversation, "I am turning on the tape recorder. I need to advise you of your rights."

Griffin smiled at the young investigator's impatience. With more experience, Keith would find that some of the best information would come from the rambling chit-chat of a suspect and that a relaxed relationship gets more information than the tones of "officialdom." *He'll learn, though,* Griffin thought. *He's a quick study.*

"Oh, I know all about *that*. We can just skip it."

"No sir, I'm afraid we can't." Keith spoke into the recorder, giving the time, date, and place of interrogation. "Mr. Calley, before talking to us, I must inform you that you have the right to remain silent—"

"Young man, if I wanted to remain silent, I wouldn't be here, would I?"

"You have the right to the presence of an attorney," Keith continued as if he had not been interrupted. "If you cannot afford an attorney, one will be appointed. If you give up these rights, anything you say can and will be used against you in a court of law."

"Yes, yes. I know. Let's get on with this."

"*However*, even if you give up these rights and begin talking, you may stop at any time, and ask for a lawyer. Do you understand all of these rights I have explained?"

"Yes, I've told you several times now." He was tapping his foot irritably.

"Do you understand that I am taping this conversation?"

"I'm not deaf, young man. Let's get on with it."

"What is your name?"

"I *told* you, it's Quinton Calley."

"How old are you, Mr. Calley?"

"I'm forty-four, if that has anything to do with it."

"What is your address, Mr. Calley?"

"Twenty-three, thirty-two Huson Street, Greenbriar, New York. I am a representative for Jocelyn cosmetics. I demonstrate the proper way to apply make-up. I am in your city for a convention of cosmetic dealers."

"Mr. Calley, would you tell us why you're here this morning?" Keith asked.

"I killed a man yesterday, cut him up into pieces, and spread his body all over your county."

"What was the man's name?"

"I have no idea."

"Where did you meet this man?"

"In a bar near the Civic Center. A trashy little place. The Merry-something-or-other."

"Would that be the Merry-Go-Round?" Griffin asked, looking at Keith with raised eyebrows.

"Yes, and yes, I *am* gay. I presume that's what you really wanted to know—by the look you gave your partner."

"Why did you kill him, Mr. Calley?"

"He tried to rob me after we . . . after our *arrangement* was over."

"What arrangement, Mr. Calley?"

"Come now, young man. I have no intention of going into the sordid details. I think you have a pretty good idea what homosexuals do when they're alone."

"How did you kill him?"

"I shot him three times with a little derringer, .22 caliber. He fell down after two shots, but I reloaded and shot him for good measure one more time."

"Where did this happen?"

"In my room at the Hilton."

"Where did the dismemberment take place?"

"In the bathtub, of course."

"What did you use?"

"If you mean what kind of tool, I used a Boy Scout knife. The kind with all the blades."

For the first time, Griffin showed interest. He interjected a question.

"What kind of blades did that knife have, Mr. Calley?"

"A big blade, a small one, a leather punch, a can opener, and a little saw."

Griffin leaned back in his chair and nodded for Keith to continue.

"What kind of transportation did you use?"

"I have a rented Oldsmobile, that I drove from the airport," the little man said.

"Do you have the pistol and the knife with you, Mr. Calley?"

"No, I threw them both in the river, when I threw the head off the bridge."

Keith glanced at Griffin. That had not been in the papers.

31

"Describe the containers you put the body parts in."

"Silver garbage bags, except for the one suitcase you found behind the church."

"Describe the suitcase."

"It was just a suitcase," the man snapped. "When are you going to have me sign the confession?"

"I need to know about the suitcase, Mr. Calley."

"Oh . . . it was brown, I think."

"Good condition? Poor? Average?"

"I don't know. I bought it at a second-hand store, for God's sake!"

"Officer Keith, I think Mr. Calley is gettin' a little tense. Why don't you walk him down to C.I.D. and have them make a picture of him."

"But—" the investigator began.

"I *really* think it would be a good idea."

"All right, Sergeant." Keith turned off the recorder. "Come with me, Mr. Calley."

When they had gone, Doyle walked out to the reception area and got a cup of coffee. He went back to his office, lit a cigarette, and called the records division.

"This is Sergeant Griffin. I need to talk to either the chief of police, or the chief of detectives in Greenbriar, New York. I'll hold."

Twenty minutes later, Doyle heard them coming back from the C.I.D. office. Keith sounded irritated.

"I'm sorry, Mr. Calley, but we don't have glamour photography here. That's the best I can do."

"I certainly hope you don't intend to *run* this in the papers. It's not even my good side."

As they came into the office, Keith tossed the Polaroids on the desk. He reached for the recorder, but Griffin held up his hand.

"Let's talk off the record a minute," the sergeant said. Keith shrugged and folded his arms. It was obvious that he thought the detective was stealing his thunder.

"Mr. Calley, do you know Chief of Detectives Simpson from up in Greenbriar, New York?"

"Oh, you've talked to *him*." Calley's voice had become icy. "I know him, but I wouldn't call him a policeman by any means."

"He knows you, too, Mr. Calley. In fact, he knows you well. He tells me that you have confessed to several crimes, including the Son of Sam killings, the Boston Strangler killings, and to being Zodiac and the Green River Killer."

"*Well*, I have no intention of being patronized by a hick policeman in a backwater town. I assure you, though, that your superiors are not going to be happy when they find out you let a butcher walk out of here. I'm going now, *Sergeant*."

"That's a good idea, Mr. Calley. Otherwise I might feel compelled to book you on suspicion and hold you until this investigation clears you. The jailers might put you in with a bunch of hairy convicts, who wouldn't appreciate your finer qualities." The little man slammed the door on his way out.

"How did you know?" Keith asked.

"I didn't *know*. We had to sit here playing cat and mouse until we were sure, though. I just short-circuited the cat and mouse part."

"How did he know about the head off the bridge?"

"Same way you did. Logical deduction. Remember, he's an expert in his own way. He's been involved in more homicides than you have."

"My apologies," Keith said.

"For what?"

"For what I was thinking."

"Come on, partner," Griffin stood up. "Let's go work this homicide. I promise you that wasn't the last confession."

Chapter Four

"What did you do wrong, Germ? There's a cop behind us with blue lights flashin'."

"I didn't do nothin' wrong, Wildman. I stopped at all the signs and lights and signaled all my turns."

Germ was not noted among the Devil's Sons for his brilliance. There had even been a rumor that it was necessary to write on the back of his hands which side was for the throttle and which for the hand-brake. He was a good soldier, though. He asked no questions.

Wildman Parker, vice-president of the local Devil's Sons chapter, looked nervously over his shoulder out the rear window of the truck as the officer approached. There was no thought of resisting or causing problems. The current biker law was to keep a low profile. Never "hassle" the man. He hoped to God, however, that neither of the Harley-Davidson motorcycles in the back of the pickup had been reported stolen. He did not think they would be, but screw-ups happen.

"What's wrong, Officer?" Germ asked in his best citizen's voice. "I done everything right. Why'd you stop me?"

"It's customary for me to ask the questions," the deputy sheriff said. "When I get all my answers, I'll be glad to answer yours. You got that?"

Oh no, Wildman thought, *we got a hardnose here.*

Most cops see outlaw bikers as no different from the others they stop. Some, however, are offended that outlaw bikers are

34

allowed to breathe the same air as everyone else. They see bikers as the epitome of everything that is wrong with the world. According to their reasoning, cops are law-abiding, take baths regularly, and look neat. Bikers are just the opposite, thus the enemy.

Such an officer had stopped them. Sheriff's Deputy David Lark despised bikers of every stripe and color. He even found his feelings for fellow officers affected if they rode Harley-Davidsons. No self-respecting outlaw rides anything but a Harley or an Indian, American made.

A hundred years before, David Lark would have turned his wrath on cattle rustlers and bank robbers. In the latter part of the twentieth century, he had outlaw bikers—dirty, filthy, scurvy gutter rats—to be driven off the face of the earth, or at least off Lark's beat.

"Both of you come out of that truck . . . slowly." Lark had not drawn his weapon, but neither biker had any doubt that he would welcome the opportunity to shoot both of them. "Keep your hands where I can see them."

"No problem, Officer," Wildman answered, "We ain't done nothin' wrong." Nevertheless, he was sweating, wondering about the two scooters. Wildman looked a lot like pictures of Rasputin, the "Mad Monk," except more bizarre. He was clad in denim trousers and a dirty leather vest, with "Devil's Sons, Tennessee" displayed on the back.

Germ looked a lot like Wildman, only on a larger scale. His jacket, however, said "Devil's Sons, Prospect." He was not a full-fledged member. After he had proved that he could rape, murder, deal dope, and had other useful outlaw traits, he would be allowed to wear a full membership patch.

"Both of you, assume the position on the bed of the truck." They did so without comment, and he patted them down for weapons.

"Walk back to my cruiser and get in the rear driver's side," he told them. Of medium height, with blond hair just short of being what had been called a crew-cut before the officer had

35

been born, he glistened when he walked, from his highly shined ankle boots to his stainless-steel spectacle frames.

"What's he doin', Wildman?"

"What's it look like he's doin', dummy? He's searchin' the truck."

"Ain't we got no constitutional rights, Wildman?"

"Shut up, Germ. Some cops figure they can't win if they play by the rules. That makes a dangerous cop for us. If we squawk, he'll find some reason to arrest us. We're enemies, and he's smart enough to know it. Just be glad there ain't nothin' illegal in the truck—and pray them two scooters is clean."

Finding nothing of interest inside, the officer ran the tag on the truck and the vehicle identification number, to see if they matched. He then climbed into the back of the truck and called in the tag numbers and VINs on the two motorcycles. In a few minutes, he apparently received word that all numbers checked clean. He made notes in his little black book, then strode back to the cruiser and opened the door.

"Which one of you is Gordon Parker?"

"I am," Wildman said. "That's my truck."

"So the computer says. Now who are the two gentlemen who own the Harleys?"

"I don't know, Officer," Wildman said. "We're just deliverin' for a shop called Scooters Unlimited." Scooters Unlimited was a front for a Devil's Sons' theft ring.

"So you don't know Larry Foglesong or William Charter?" the deputy asked.

"No sir."

"Both of you, break out some identification." They complied, and he stood looking at the drivers' licenses, then at them, matching pictures with faces.

"What's your street name, Parker?"

"I only got one name. Gordon Parker."

"Parker," the deputy leaned down until his nose was almost against the biker's cheek, "I feel an arrest coming on. *What is your street name?*" Every biker has a street name. As with

36

many Indian tribes, each member is rechristened after joining the club.

"It's Wildman. That's Germ beside me."

"My, what an apt name for your friend. Did anyone ever tell you that you look like Rasputin?"

"Yessir."

"Both of you, get out of my cruiser so I can disinfect it. Take off!"

They got out of the cruiser and walked towards the old truck. Curiosity got the better of Germ.

"Officer, why did you stop me?"

"Because," Deputy Lark smiled a wolflike smile, "I saw you drive away from the clubhouse. In my log, though, it will say you were stopped for 'obstructing traffic.' If you wish to complain, I'll be more than glad to give you my badge number and name."

"No sir, we don't need that at all. No problem," Wildman answered.

"I told you to shut up, Germ! If he had been in the mood, we'd both be wearin' cuffs. Some cops you can talk back to, some you can't. You'd better learn the difference."

"Sorry, Wildman."

"No harm done, I guess. Everything's cool."

Wildman was wrong, of course, but it would be a while before he knew it.

"Hey, Sherry, come here."

Curt Monroe leaned back in his ragged easy chair, holding the newspaper in his left hand and a Budweiser with the other. Short, unshaven, and overweight, he was dressed for his work as a construction laborer, but his clothes were still clean at four-thirty in the afternoon. There had been no work at the union hall that morning, so he had done what he usually did: he sat around a nearby tavern with other unemployed union laborers.

The union was the best thing that had ever happened to him. Time was when he had worked as a nonunion laborer with great regularity, but at lower wages. Then a friend had wrangled a union card for him, letting him earn twice as much per hour. His income, however, was down by more than 50 percent, because the union kept him employed less than half the time. He found it a satisfactory situation.

He had never married Sherry and had never acknowledged her two children as his own. Therefore she was able to draw a welfare check on both of them, as well as other federal benefits. His occasional forays into the construction trade brought in enough for his beer and cigarettes. When someone asked him why an able-bodied man was lying around, not working, he would tell them the union hadn't found him anything.

"Whatta ya want?" She stood at the door, hair stringy, dress dingy, and feet bare. At twenty-eight, she looked fifty. She saw no reason to make any effort to look better. A second generation welfare recipient, she could not imagine a better life.

"Look at this picture in the *Journal*."

"So?" She glanced at the sketch, pushing a strand of hair out of her eyes.

"It looks like the Donkey."

"No, it don't. And don't call him the Donkey. He wuz always nice to me." She did not add that the man they were discussing might be the real father of her older daughter.

"Come on," Curt chuckled, "the guy's a moron." Monroe's own I.Q. was between seventy-five and eighty, and he had quit the seventh grade at the age of sixteen.

"He's not! Larry's slow on account of the motorcycle wreck, but he ain't stupid. And he never beat me, either!"

"Come on! I *know* why you kept him around so long. It didn't have nothin' to do with him bein' nice. The Donkey only had one thing goin' for him!"

"That's a lie! Anyway, that picture don't look like him."

"Sure it does," Curt insisted. "Look at the shape of the face and the mustache."

"Larry's nowhere near that heavy," she said, moving in for a closer look.

"Dontcha think that maybe it would've swelled a little after he was dead for a while?"

"Does it say 'bout a scar on his left arm?" She shuddered as a vision of the bodiless head crossed her mind.

"They ain't found the arms yet. It's him. It's the Donkey," Curt Monroe insisted.

"No," she hugged herself and shivered, "nobody'd want to kill Larry. He wuz gentle as a lamb."

"Yeah, but don't forget—he was like a donkey, too." Curt chuckled at his own wit.

"Personally, I think it's a lot of hullabaloo over nothin'," Mike Patterson, also known as "Jumbo," said. "I think it was a domestic that got out of hand. His ole lady kept tellin' him to carry out the garbage. He kept ignorin' her until she lost her temper. Then she carried him out *with* the garbage."

"You always wanna complicate things, Jumbo. It wasn't a domestic dispute. It was a suicide. The guy went around lopping off body parts. The last to go was the head. He put the bag over his head before he ditched his arms and *rolled* the three miles to the river. If Lieutenant Freeman was still here, he'd have closed the case by now," George Poplin taunted, taking a swig of draught beer and wiping his mouth with the back of his hand. George was among the smaller officers of the Horton County Sheriff's Department. He was called, naturally, "Midget."

Lieutenant Harold Freeman, a retired homicide investigator, had been notorious for closing homicide cases by calling them suicides.

His most famous case had concerned a man shot square in the back of the head with a thirty ought six rifle. Freeman extrapolated that the victim had stood on his bed, wedged the rifle between his head and the wall, reached back and pushed the trigger with his thumb, then managed to fall into a perfect fetal position, with the rifle falling off the bed, ten feet away.

He might have gotten away with it, had the victim's brother not been smitten by an attack of conscience, which brought forth a tearful confession.

After that day he was called "Suicide" Freeman. Horton County cops swore that killers from all over the country came to their county to commit murders while Freeman was working.

"You know, that reminds me of a case I responded to once," Gary Keith said. The investigator was unwinding from his case, going into its third day with an unidentified victim.

"Here it comes," Jumbo giggled, straightening his 300-pound bulk in the chair. "College Boy is gonna enthrall us with one of his stories. They always sound *so* much more interestin' when *he* tells them."

"Listen up, Jumbo," Midget told him. "You might learn somethin', far-fetched though it seems."

"I answered a suicide-in-progress call a few years ago," Keith said, ignoring Jumbo's comment. "It's a two-story house. The husband meets me at the door, hysterical. He says his old lady has locked herself in upstairs and that she's been really depressed. He says he heard her thrashing around on the floor.

"We went up and the door was locked from the inside. It was a heavy door, and it took us twenty minutes to break it down. His wife is on the floor, her head is almost completely severed, and there's a big butcher knife beside her."

"Let me guess," Midget said. "Freeman came and declared it a suicide."

"No. Freeman had us load the poor guy as soon as he got there. While he's browbeating the husband, I check the windows. They're locked from the *inside*. I *knew* the door was locked, and with a deadbolt.

"I checked the woman's hands. There were no cuts at all, no kind of mark to indicate that she was defending herself. While Freeman was trying to extract a confession from the husband, I waited around with Criminalistics. They treated her hand and put it under ultraviolet light. There was the imprint of the back of the butcher knife across her palms.

"When Freeman finally got around to calling the woman's psychiatrist, he finds that the woman has fits of episodic psychosis of a type that renders a person almost impervious to pain. The woman *did* cut her own throat, almost decapitated herself."

"Boy," Jumbo said, "that husband sho' was lucky she locked the door."

"Yeah, things are not always what they seem," Keith reflected as he sipped his scotch and soda. Everyone else was drinking beer.

"Are you saying," Midget asked, "that this corpse has faked its own death?" He belched loudly. Everyone ignored him.

"You're all off track," David Lark said. He had been sitting at the table, quietly listening to the conversation. "It's an outlaw biker, revenge killing. We'll find the Devil's Sons at the bottom of this. Mark my words."

"You're nuts about outlaw bikers," Jumbo snorted. "You probably think they did the Lindberg kidnapping."

"Laugh all you want, Jumbo. But mark my words, the bikers did it."

"It was a black mass," Hank Pike said.

They all turned to stare at him. He was a laconic, laid-back cop of forty, notorious for doing as little as possible on the streets. Sometimes, he would drink all evening without joining the conversation.

"Halloween's coming up day after tomorrow. The guy was killed in some sort of pre-Halloween ritual. We can look for another killin' on Halloween."

"Like an adult version of trick or treat," Jumbo said, taking a swig of beer. The group broke into hysterical laughter. Any joke would seem funny now, since they were into their fifth round of drinks.

"Well, one thing for sure," Midget insisted. "Laying all

jokes aside, whoever did it was bright, very bright. He's pulled off a murder right under our noses, and we don't have a clue."

"I'll drink to that," Gary Keith agreed.

They all drank to that, then to motherhood, apple pie, and Willie Nelson. At some point they began to drink to the letters of the alphabet. This time, Keith stayed until the letter *K*.

Chapter Five

Doyle Griffin sat at his potter's wheel, "throwing" a delicate tea cup. He never ceased to be amazed how a thing of beauty could arise from a lump of clay. It was really his only source of relaxation. He had dug the clay, a mixture of soft grays and reds, from the banks of the Holston River himself.

Doyle's friends would have been surprised to know about his hobby. Although he seemed to have an uncanny knack for finding beautiful ceramic pieces, which he often gave as Christmas and birthday gifts, no one at the department knew that he turned them himself.

His mind was occupied as his fingers shaped the clay. Hank Pike was not the only person who had realized that Halloween was approaching. While Doyle did not really expect another killing, he felt that Halloween would make things difficult.

He had already received two phone calls from people who had heard rumors that the sheriff's department was investigating a cult that sacrificed children as a part of their ritual. Also, a woman had called to demand that a psychic be brought in to solve the case. There was, she said, a famous psychic nearby in Asheville working on a string of rape-murders.

Doyle had heard of the woman psychic, who billed herself as "Samantha." He had, in fact, researched her in the past. Most of her "predictions," it seemed to him, were given *after* the case was solved. But she had a loyal following.

He was so involved with the case that he did not hear his living room door open quietly.

A figure slipped in and eased the door shut, a hideous skeleton mask covering the head. Slowly and quietly the figure disrobed in the semidark living room. On tiptoes the masked figure approached the extra bedroom where the detective had his studio. The soft hum of the wheel was the only sound.

With a blood-curdling scream, the intruder leaped through the door landing in front of Doyle. The arms were above the head, the legs spread wide, revealing a totally naked body.

"I've heard of puttin' a bag over the head," Doyle said calmly, as he adjusted the side of the tea cup he was making, "but in this case, I think maybe the bag is worse than the face behind it."

"Bastard," the apparition swore, pulling the rubber mask over her head. "Does anything ever frighten you?"

Dark hair cascaded down her back. She was a compact woman, twenty-five or so, the type of woman that men remember as beautiful, even when she is not. Her body was firm, the breasts small enough to have eluded the damage of gravity. Her hips, which flared more widely than some men would have liked, were products of her Slavic ancestry, the same genes that gave her almost almond-shaped eyes.

"Yeah," he stood and raised his clay covered hands, "the idea of old age scares me to death." He started toward her, hands extended.

"Don't you touch me with that junk all over your hands," she retreated, giggling.

"Too late," he said, pinning her to the wall. His hands cupped her buttocks as he kissed her. In a moment, her breasts were also smeared with the red and gray clay. Picking her up, he carried her to his bedroom.

Later they sat at the table, drinking coffee.

"I hope you didn't get any of that junk in my hair. I go on in forty-five minutes."

"Trish, I really wasn't concentratin' on your hair. I've got an idea, though. Why don't you go on the air in that costume Halloween night? I guarantee it would raise the ratings."

"I don't think so," she said. "How would it affect the image of a cool, sophisticated newswoman to appear naked?"

"I guess we'll never know. Probably wouldn't hurt you any more than havin' everyone find out that you sleep with a cop."

"I'd say you're right, Officer. People in the circles I inhabit do not socialize with sadistic fascists."

"That's all right, Trish. People in my circles don't deal with bubble-headed intellectuals who live in ivory towers."

"It's a stand-off then." She walked into the living room to recover her clothes. "I'm off Halloween. You wanna spend the night at my place?"

"Can't. We'll be covered up with prank calls about the torso. And we might just get lucky and get a real one."

"Well, if you'd rather work than have *this*," she patted her behind, "that's entirely up to you."

"Breaks of the game," he shrugged, lighting a cigarette.

The sheriff's deputy got out of the car and slammed the door in irritation. The accident call had been dispatched at ten minutes before shift change. Now he would be late getting off. To make matters worse, a well-dressed woman of fifty or so was shrilly berating a man who stood with his head down. One of his arms hung limply at his side.

"I'm Officer Tolliver." He was already sketching the position of the vehicles. "I need both of the drivers to come and pull the vehicles off the road."

"Aren't you going to take measurements, Officer?" The pudgy woman forgot about the man she had been abusing, turning her wrath on the officer.

"There's no need for measurements. It's a rear-end collision. *This* vehicle," he pointed to the late-model Buick, "struck *that* vehicle in the rear. The accident occurred at a red light, where vehicles normally stop. The accident is self-explanatory. Now, both of you move your vehicles over to that parking lot, out of traffic."

"It most certainly is *not* self-explanatory! That old beat-up

Chevrolet has no brake lights. If he had brake lights, I never would have hit him."

"Did you not see the red light, ma'am?" Tolliver, an immaculately dressed patrolman with bushy brown hair and mustache, was tired and irritated.

"Young man, I don't intend to stand here and take sarcasm from someone whose salary is paid by my taxes!"

"And I have no intention of standing here and arguing with a cheapskate who pays me such a paltry salary. Get your car off the road before I hook a wrecker up to it!" She had hit a sore spot, having no idea how many times Tolliver had heard that particular statement in his career.

Without further argument, she huffed to the car and pulled into the lot of a Kentucky Fried Chicken restaurant. Tolliver pointed to the lot, and the disabled man limped to his old Chevrolet. For the first time, Tolliver saw the mousy woman sitting in the passenger seat.

"I need to see an operator's license and a car registration from both of you," the officer said.

Indignantly, the pudgy woman shoved the paperwork toward Tolliver. He recorded the needed information and handed it back. The man with the crippled arm shuffled over and handed him a driver's license and registration. The officer examined the documents.

"A Larry Foglesong is listed as the owner of this vehicle, Mr. Courtney. Did you purchase this car from him?"

"No, sir," the man mumbled, eyes downcast. Partially paralyzed on the right side, he was nonetheless solid looking. At thirty-six years old, his hair had receded to fuzz on top. "The car still belongs to Larry. He lent it to me."

"You need to inform him immediately so he can inform his insurance company," Tolliver said, filling in the blanks on the accident report.

"Officer!" The pudgy woman had held her peace as long as possible. "If I am not badly mistaken, the law requires that a person carry proof of insurance at all times."

"You *are* mistaken," Tolliver retorted. "Tennessee does not have a mandatory insurance law. The owner of the vehicle must either meet his obligations or lose his tags. The insurance is a matter between the two car owners."

"In other words, the riff-raff can run around, taking no responsibility whatsoever, while people like me and my husband work ourselves to death. I *demand* that you cite this man for not having brake lights!"

The woman had just uttered another word one does not bring up to tired, irritated patrol officers. In doing so, she had assured there would be a citation.

"Get in the car and hit the brakes, Mr. Courtney," Tolliver said. He waited as the man complied. Both brake lights came on.

"They were not working when he made the sudden stop in front of me!" the woman said shrilly.

Without speaking, the officer went back to his cruiser and returned with a citation book. The woman looked gloatingly at the crippled man as Tolliver filled in the blanks. Her smug expression vanished as the officer extended the citation book to her. "Sign here. This is not an admission of guilt, only an agreement to appear in court."

"You're giving me a citation? For *what?*"

"For following too closely. It's marked. Sign on the bottom line," Tolliver said.

"I most certainly will *not* sign. I'd rather go to jail first."

"That's good," Tolliver said with a smile, "because that's exactly where you're going, if you don't sign the citation. A citation is an agreement to appear without bond."

"You wouldn't *dare*. You don't know who my husband is," she said. "He'd have your badge."

"Try me, lady. I don't *care* who your husband is. If he was the *sheriff* of this county, you'd get the ticket after the way you've behaved. Sign it now, or put your hands on the side of my cruiser!"

The woman signed the ticket, almost cutting through all five layers. Tolliver was glad. He really did not want to jail anyone—not after quitting time. He might get a complaint.

Maybe not, though. The woman's husband probably disliked her as much as everyone else did. He noticed that the purple of her enraged face clashed with her blue-tinted hair. Stalking to the car, she got in and drove away, nose in the air, staring straight ahead.

"You can go now," Tolliver told the man with the crippled arm who was watching quietly from a distance. "Make sure you notify the owner that his car has been involved in an accident." Getting into his cruiser, Tolliver pulled away, glad it had not taken any longer. He was running only twenty minutes late.

The man with the crippled arm walked slowly back to the car and got in. He sat staring ahead for a minute, then started the old Chevrolet.

"I told you we shouldn't be drivin' this car," the mousy woman said, her mouth drawn in a tight line. She had not been pretty at twenty, and at forty-five she was hard. A stroke two years earlier had left her with little movement on the right side of her face.

"Whatta ya wanna do, walk?"

"Naw, but we shouldn't be drivin' this car."

"You worry too much. This car ain't been stole. There's nobody lookin' for it!"

"I don't care. I told you we shouldn't drive it."

"Aw, the hell with ya!"

"When did you first realize you had this spiritual gift, Samantha?" The interviewer, a brittle looking woman of indeterminate age, leaned forward and gazed intently at her guest. Cynthia Whittle had long ago given up hope of being picked up by a major network, so she worked hard at hosting a local television variety show. Asheville, North Carolina, was not the entertainment capital of the world, but there were worse places to work.

"I was twelve, Cynthia." Samantha Thorpe's soft accent placed her near the Charleston, South Carolina, area. "I went into a walking trance and saw a plane crash in Columbia, two days before it happened."

"So you don't have to be focused on a particular subject to pick up vibrations?"

"Not at all," Samantha said, tossing her head to move the long, blue-black hair from her face. Worn in a style popular in Samantha's high school days, the hairdo had looked good on her when she was sixteen. Now at forty, it looked ridiculous. Her dark eye make-up, red lipstick, and pale complexion gave her the appearance of a witch in a second-rate Hollywood drama. She had to keep her chin lifted at all times to prevent sagging on her neck.

"In other words, things just *come* to you at times?"

"That's right, Cynthia. Generally I *invoke* a trance by having an object associated with the case near me, but at times, vibrations of an incident are so strong that it just takes me over, so to speak."

"This is really amazing," Cynthia said. "For those of you who just tuned in, I am interviewing Samantha Thorpe, world famous psychic from South Carolina." She turned back to her guest. "Samantha, what would you say was your most interesting case to date?"

Samantha did not answer. Her eyes seemed to be focused on a point beyond the room. They were blinking rapidly, and her jaw muscles were writhing.

"Something seems to be happening here," Cynthia Whittle said, leaning closer to her guest. "Can you hear me, Samantha?"

"Jigsaw, jigsaw, jigsaw . . ." Samantha chanted quietly, eyes burning in their sockets.

"This is amazing," Cynthia Whittle said. "We may be witnessing the *first* psychic trance on *any* variety show, ever." Cynthia knew how to handle unexpected circumstances.

"They've turned him into a jigsaw puzzle," Samantha said in a sing-song voice.

"Who? Where?" Cynthia asked dramatically.

"In the city of Horton, by the two rivers, they gathered. Chanting to darkness, they made him into a jigsaw puzzle. It's an old word . . . an Indian word . . . ," Samantha intoned. "Tanasi."

"Tennessee? Did you say Tennessee, Samantha? Horton, Tennessee? Somebody get an atlas. This is *amazing!*" Cynthia interjected. "My guest, Samantha Thorpe, has gone into a trance before our eyes."

"More! More! More! There will be more!" Samantha, chanted, seeming on the verge of hysteria. "More silver garbage bags! More jigsaw people! The darkness *must be stopped!*" Samantha collapsed, and the director went to a commercial break.

"Ladies and gentlemen, I have never encountered such an experience in all my years in broadcasting. Ten minutes ago, before our very eyes, Samantha Thorpe, who is in our city to work with the police on a murder case, went into a trance. We have that trance on tape.

"I am doing what I have never done before. With apologies to my other guests, I have canceled them to concentrate on Samantha's experience here." Cynthia leaned forward, speaking earnestly to the television audience.

"I am going to briefly recap what happened, then play the tape of the incident. Afterwards, if Samantha is up to it, we'll bring her back out.

"A few minutes ago, Samantha went into a trance. She chanted, 'Jigsaw, jigsaw, jigsaw.' Moments later she said there would be more jigsaw people. She said the words *Horton, by the two rivers,* then a word, which we have clarified by playing the tape back. The word was *Tanasi.*

"Samantha went on to warn that there would be others. She said, 'More jigsaw people. More silver garbage bags.' Then Samantha collapsed.

"Checking the atlas, my staff found a city and county called Horton. This county is in the state of Tennessee. This is the eerie part, ladies and gentlemen. The word that Samantha

50

uttered, *Tanasi,* is an old Indian word. The modern English word, *Tennessee,* is a corruption of *Tanasi.*

"The news staff here at Channel 3 called a television station in Horton. The news staff has informed me that there has indeed been a murder in Horton, Tennessee. A body was cut into segments. These segments were placed around the county in *silver* garbage bags.

"It staggers the imagination, friends. The news staff also tells me that this story was not publicized in our city, where Samantha has been for the last two days, nor was it publicized nationally.

"Bear this in mind as you watch the tape of Samantha's trance. There seems to be no rational explanation!"

As the tape was playing, Samantha Thorpe was escorted back into the studio by a member of the staff. Her legs seemed to be shaky. When the tape ended, Cynthia was ready. Dramatically she turned to her guest.

"Samantha, do you feel strong enough to continue?"

Samantha nodded, chin uplifted, and shook her hair over her shoulder.

"Samantha, have you ever been in Horton, Tennessee, or had you ever heard of the murder before tonight?"

"No. To both questions."

"Did you read or hear *anything* about Horton, Tennessee, before tonight?"

"No, Cynthia. Let me say this, though. As painful and as powerful as the experience was, if the police in Horton ask for my assistance, I will go there, as I have done so many times in my life when the police were at a dead end."

"There you have it, friends. This courageous woman has offered her help to the police in Horton, Tennessee, a place she had not even been aware of until tonight. Let's see what they have to say about it."

Samantha Thorpe could have passed a lie detector on the questions she was asked: She had *not* been in Horton, Tennessee, *nor* had she heard of the murder *before* that evening, when one of her fans tracked her down by telephone just before the taping of the show. The loyal follower had given her all the grisly details. It was the same woman, in fact, who had called Doyle Griffin to demand that he seek Samantha's help.

Samantha had answered all of the interviewer's questions to the technical letter. The psychic had no bookings for the remainder of the month, and Horton was not too far away, just across the Hot Springs Mountains. She did not charge fees, of course, for her "gift," but the publicity always brought in a lot of readings and sold a few more copies of her self-published book.

The television interview was picked up by the national networks and people in Horton, who never even read newspapers, saw and heard about the "Jigsaw Man." Doyle cursed and refused to make comments, as did Gary Keith. A medical examiner did talk to the television cameras—and lived to regret it.

Cynthia Whittle was not picked up by a major network.

Chapter Six

Glen Moffit had dreamed of being a police officer when he was growing up. He could not remember a time when men in blue uniforms, wearing shiny badges, had not filled him with awe. More than anything else, he wanted to be a policeman. He had envied the middle-class kids with whom he attended school. They could do anything they wanted. Glen could not. That is to say, Glen could not muster enough courage to tell his mother that he wanted to be a cop, not a doctor. Hardly anyone ever found enough courage to argue with his mother.

So Glen Moffit became a doctor. It was only natural, given his bent, that he became a specialist in forensic medicine. Eventually, he became a medical examiner for the coroner's office. As an assistant coroner, he had a badge of his own. If it were flashed quickly enough, people would often mistake it for a real cop's badge. Once a couple of detectives had even invited him to go drinking with them. He had failed to show up at a party given by the mayor in order to go. He treasured the evening, though it was never repeated. He would gladly have given up his practice to be a cop, making only 20 percent of his annual salary.

When the reporters called for the coroner, Glen had to tell them that the coroner was in Baltimore at a convention. When they asked who was second in command, he modestly admitted that he was. When they asked for a few words about the Jigsaw Man, he was overwhelmed by temptation.

An hour later, the reporters had gathered around him. He smiled nervously, a round little man with fine blond hair and a cherubic face. He did not realize that the press was thrashing about in desperation, because the sheriff's department had put a lid on information.

"Dr. Moffit, what part have you played in this investigation?" The reporter was a petite blonde who incited lust in Moffit.

"Well . . . I was the medical examiner on the scene when the body parts were first discovered."

"Doctor, there has been some confusion about the exact cause of death in this case. Can you clarify for us?"

"Well . . . there were three rounds of .22 caliber ammunition in the chest cavity and a wound inflicted by a sharp instrument in the eye socket. Either could have caused death."

"Which would *you* say caused death, Doctor?"

"Well, it would seem . . ." The petite blonde was causing a malfunction in his normally quick thought processes. "Rather, I would imagine that he was shot first. Most killers use a firearm if it's available to them. On the other hand—"

"Doctor, was this body cut apart by a person skilled with surgical tools and familiar with anatomy?"

"That would be hard to say."

"In *your* opinion, Doctor?"

"Well, it was done at least partly by a fine-toothed saw and a very sharp knife—"

"Such as a surgical saw and scalpel?"

"That's one possibility, but—"

"So, in effect, Doctor, there's a possibility that this unidentified man was murdered by a person very familiar with surgical techniques?"

"Anything is possible, but —"

"Thank you, Doctor. You've been very helpful."

As Glen Moffit watched the reporters depart to make a deadline, he tried to remember exactly what he had said, or not said. His questions were cleared up by the morning newspaper:

CORONER SAYS JIGSAW KILLER MAY HAVE USED SURGICAL TOOLS

An assistant coroner for Horton County says that the killer of a man found scattered in silver garbage bags around the county possibly shot the victim before dismembering him and may have possessed surgical skills, perhaps using precision instruments in the dismemberment . . . .

John Waters used his key to let himself into the apartment. It was, as usual, dark. Sarah did not like bright light. Her aversion to it had grown in the two years that he had known her.

He stood, letting his eyes adjust to the dark. Eventually, in the dim glow of the small night light across the room he saw the fluorescent symbols of the zodiac on the wall behind the bed. He could hear Sarah's breathing from the bed, even and quiet.

The room was a monument to the occult. On the wall across from the zodiac was a plaque depicting the two-faced god Janus. On a table stood a two-foot statue of Pan, holding his pipes before him. A shelf on one side of the kitchen contained a rack of herbs, giving the apartment a pungent odor.

In the room off the kitchen, which had once been a dining room, a circle was permanently in place on the floor, made of ribbon, glued down. In the center of the circle was a pentagram, like the one Sarah had given him to wear around his neck. A small altar sat in the center. On it was a chalice, a censer, a reed wand, and a double-edged dagger.

John walked to the refrigerator and opened it. Despite the rest of the apartment, it was an ordinary refrigerator, with everyday food. Opening the freezer compartment, he deposited a package wrapped in butcher paper.

In a few moments, he stood by the bed, looking down at Sarah as he removed his clothes. The plastic bag on the bedside table explained why she was sleeping so soundly. Marijuana spilled out onto the table top.

Sarah was a big woman, blonde and robust. This was fine

with John. He was a big man, with hulking shoulders. Sarah's hair, worn in braids wrapped around her head, made her look like a Viking maiden. It was the hair and her size that had attracted him to her one night at the community college where he was taking a course in livestock breeding.

He slipped into the bed, pulling back the sheet that was covering her. She moved and moaned softly as he pressed his face against her. Lifting John in her arms, she pulled him on top of her, adjusting her body to his as they merged.

Minutes later, they both shuddered and he rolled over on his back.

"Hello," she said sleepily.

"Hello, yourself. What have you been doin' today?"

"I had a couple of clients. One needed a love potion. The other thinks she has cancer."

"Did you fix them up?"

"Of course. That's why I'm here," she said.

"I still have trouble with the idea of healin' people in the dark," John said.

"That's because you still think in terms of good and evil. Neither exists, love, only power. Power is neither good nor evil. It just *is*."

"My upbringin', I guess."

"Of all people, you should know that what people *do*, not what they *say*, is important. Your father was one of the best examples I ever heard of."

"I guess you're right."

"Did you bring the package?"

"Yeah, it's in the freezer—liver, heart, and the sweetbread."

"Oooh!" she said, making a kissing sound with her lips. "That should make a *lovely* meal."

"Right there," the trembling woman said, "behind the rose bush."

Jumbo Patterson threw the beam of his rechargeable flashlight on the silver garbage bag behind the rose bush. It was slit on the side and what appeared to be blood was spilling out.

"How did you happen to notice this bag, ma'am?"

"Someone beat on the door, then ran away. When I looked out, it was on the porch. I picked it up and blood dripped out, and I threw it as far away as I could. That's where it landed!" The woman looked like a face on the end of a stick, her clothes hanging limply all over her body.

"Have you had trouble with the neighborhood kids?"

"Yes, I have, Officer. Are you gonna look in that bag or not?" To Jumbo, it was easy to see why she had trouble with neighborhood kids. Every neighborhood has a woman or man like her: dried up, unpleasant — and a perfect target.

Tiredly, Jumbo went over and untied the bag. Although he recoiled from the smell, he pulled it open. Intestines, long and looped with yellow fat mixed in, spilled out on the ground.

"Aaaagh!" He gagged, stepping back from the sight. The face on a stick walked to the other side of the porch and threw up.

"Alpha 11 to dispatch, I need a homicide officer out here to take a look at this bag."

"Is it, is it . . ." the thin woman began.

"I don't know," the big officer replied, "but whatever it is, it's ripe."

As he stood there, two young boys came from across the street and started into the yard, looking curiously at the police cruiser and the bag.

"Outta the yard," Jumbo yelled. "Go on home. This is police business."

"We just wanna look," one of them said. He was blond, thin, and a cynical-looking twelve-year-old. The other was darker but cut from the same mold.

"Out of the yard!" Jumbo repeated. "Go on home, now!"

They walked slowly back to the edge of the road and turned. "You can make us get out of the yard, but you can't make us get out of the street, lard ass!" the blond kid taunted.

"I can boot your asses about two hundred yards up the

road." When the 300-pound-plus officer started toward them, they ran like gazelles, screaming curses over their shoulders.

The neighborhood had once been quiet and totally rural. Mobile homes, however, had been moved in ten or fifteen years earlier, and their owners tended to drive pickup trucks with shotguns in the windows. Rugged individualists.

In a few minutes the two boys returned, followed by a man with a big belly in a white T-shirt. "What's the problem down here?" he demanded. "My boy says you threatened him!"

"There's not any problem. Your boy was trying to trample on a crime scene. I told him to leave."

"You can use a little manners," the man retorted. "We pay taxes the same as people in ritzy houses, but we never see cops except when there's trouble." The man was unshaven, and his words were slurred. As he got louder, lights started to come on. Other rugged individualists began to come out of their trailers.

"Your kids wouldn't understand manners, because they've never been taught any," Jumbo snarled. He was not noted for his tact. "I'll tell you the same thing I told the boys. Go home and mind your own business. Now!"

"You don't order me around, bub!"

"Try this for size, then. Get outta my sight before I load you for disorderly conduct."

"I'd like to see you try that, lard ass!"

The man in the white T-shirt, with the big belly, was surprised at how fast the 300-pound-plus cop moved. The man threw a punch, which was swept aside by a hand the size of a Virginia ham. Jumbo partly carried, partly dragged, him to the cruiser, where he cuffed him.

The stick woman ran into the house and dialed 911. By the time Doyle Griffin arrived, the three patrolmen on the scene had arrested four of the rugged individualists. Their wives and children, along with twenty or thirty other bystanders, were gathered in a semicircle threatening riot.

"Where's the bag?" Doyle asked, looking at the crowd.

"Over behind the rose bush," Jumbo replied.

"What brought this on?" Doyle nodded at the crowd.

"Just a neighborhood committee, apparently not satisfied with the police protection they receive."

Doyle squatted by the bag, wrinkling his nose at the odor. Taking out his pocket knife, he probed among the intestines as Jumbo watched from a distance. In a few minutes he stood up.

"Is it part of the puzzle?" Jumbo asked.

"Not unless the victim had a beak and feet with scales on them," Doyle replied. "This is a bag of chicken entrails and assorted parts. You've been had."

Up on the hill, above the trailer, two twelve-year-old boys giggled to themselves. They had never stirred up so much excitement before. Tomorrow was Halloween, and they were going to have a blast.

One of them was a little disturbed that his father had been arrested for disorderly conduct, but, after all, it was not the first time and probably would not be the last.

Chapter Seven

Doyle Griffin picked up the telephone in annoyance. "Homicide," he growled, then smiled as he recognized the voice.

"What's goin' on, Frank? I hope the Horton Police Department's farin' better than we are. We've got three people screening the calls, but one of us stays tied up most of the time, anyway. . . ."

"A hacksaw, wire-cutters, ice pick, a fish fillet knife, and a pair of gloves in a paper bag? . . . Under the Thurman Avenue viaduct? . . . Probably not, Frank, but I'll send someone to pick them up."

He lit a cigarette and turned to Gary Keith. "Couple of kids found a paper bag full of possible cutting tools."

"Probably nothing," Keith responded, "if the coroner's right about the surgical tools."

"Thing is, Gary, I don't recall him sayin' that to us, only the press. I ain't a doctor, but I think I could cut up a body as neat as this one was cut up. I know a good butcher could."

"You think maybe Dr. Moffit let his mouth override his good judgment?" The investigator pushed his wire-rimmed glasses upward with his thumb.

"Better men than him have come down with camera fever. If you don't care, go over to the city and get those tools before you go home. I gotta couple stops to make on my way out today."

"Sure," Keith said to the lanky sergeant as the phone rang again. "Homicide, Investigator Keith."

"Yes, I'm investigating that murder. May I have your name, please? All right, Mrs. Waters, go ahead. . . .

"You say your son threw away clothes with blood all over them, and that you've found silver garbage bags? Do you have any other reason to suspect your son of doing such a thing, Mrs. Waters? Does he have a history of emotional problems?

"You say his girlfriend practices black magic? How do you know that, Mrs. Waters?" He listened quietly, taking notes.

"A lot of people wear pentagrams, Mrs. Waters, and use herbs for medicine. . . . Have you ever been in this room you're talking about, Mrs. Waters? I'm afraid we couldn't just go in without permission. . . .

"No, I can't get up there right now, but someone will come as soon as possible. Tomorrow is Halloween, and I plan on resting tonight. Just give me your address. . . ."

"Where are you goin' at this time of night?" Curt Monroe asked Sherry, as he sipped from a can of Budweiser.

"The kids are outta milk," Sherry answered.

"If Bobby's workin' tonight, trade in some food stamps for a coupla packs of cigarettes."

"The stamps are for food. If Bobby gets caught, he'll cause Mr. Harris to lose his license," she replied.

"Don't give me a song and a dance," he snarled. "Just come back with cigarettes!"

She slammed the door behind her and walked briskly down the shaky wooden steps. The house was fifty years old and had seen little maintenance. Curt was getting worse all the time, and she was considering throwing him out. He ate and drank more than he brought in.

They had enough milk to last another day, but Sherry wanted out of the house. She had spent the last two days looking at the picture of the dead man in the *Journal*. The more she looked at it, the more it looked like her former lover. Curt had been right. Allowing for swelling, it was his twin.

A middle class American would have immediately picked up the phone and called the sheriff's department. However, Sherry was part of welfare America, with an inherent distrust of police. It had been a struggle.

She stopped at a battered phone booth and dropped in a coin. All the glass was broken out, and the phone book had long since disappeared. Sherry, however, had copied the police number from the paper.

"Hello, I got information on the jigsaw murder. . . ." Almost everyone was calling it that. "No. I don't wanna leave my name. I just wanna talk to a detective. I think I know who the dead man is."

Fidgeting in the booth, she waited impatiently, wondering if the police had some magic means to track her by telephone. She was about to hang up when Gary Keith came on the line.

"Yeah, I got information. Write down this name: Larry Foglesong. I usta live with him. He's twenty-nine years old. Last I heard he was livin' at Hartford Towers. You know, where old folks and retarded people live. . . .

"Well, he ain't really retarded, but he ain't too smart neither. He wrecked a motorcycle a few years ago and ain't been right since. He gets Social Security. . . .

"I think it's him because it *looks* like him. . . . No I ain't leavin' my name!" She hung up in a panic. It had taken all her courage to call the police. Curt would kill her if he knew.

At the office, Gary Keith sat quietly, considering what he had heard. The dead man had definitely suffered a serious head injury some years before. It was something to check out, but he was tired, and there was so much that needed checking.

He intended to pick up the cutting tools at the city police department and go home. But the best laid plans of mice and men . . .

Mark and Joanne Golden walked hand in hand by the river as the small, white dog ranged ahead of them, sniffing for signs of other dogs and putting his mark on every tree and bush he came to.

"I don't know why we had second thoughts about moving here," Joanne said. She was pushing forty-five but was the type of woman who made twenty-year-olds turn their heads when she passed, a regal woman who never became disheveled.

"I know," her husband said, "it's been wonderful away from the New York City rat race." He was about the same age as his wife, but looked older. Twenty years in the corporate law jungles had aged him. Now he wrote wills and tried misdemeanors. He was satisfied.

Mark had first discovered the rolling green mountains of East Tennessee while on a convention in Gatlinburg. After a vacation there, they had made plans to move. It had taken six months, but it had been worth it.

"What's Jingle into?" Joanne asked.

"I don't know, but let's check it out. Maybe he's cornered a rabbit."

Approaching the river bank, they saw that the poodle was taking turns pulling at a silver garbage bag and yelping excitedly. The corner of the bag tore as the couple approached.

"Come here, Jingle," Mark said, leaning down to pick up the dog. The silver garbage bag was hung in the underbrush. Suddenly the man recoiled, staggering backwards.

"What's wrong?" Joanne was alarmed.

"A snake, I think, crawling out of the bag." He stepped back for a closer look. The moonlight made the area almost as bright as day.

"Be careful," the woman warned. "It might be poisonous."

"It's . . . not a snake. It came out through a tear in the bag."

"If it's not a snake, what is it?" She asked her husband, who was trying to hold the excited poodle.

"Look for yourself."

The woman eased herself down to the edge of the water and peered closer. "My God!" she said almost reverently.

A human penis had emerged from the tear made by the

dog's teeth. Caught in the eddying waters at the river bank, it waved back and forth in the water.

"Can you believe the size of it," the sophisticated woman exclaimed. "And in *cold* water at that!"

Chapter Eight

Sammy Turpin carried in the last of the suitcases. Of the five, one contained all the belongings he had taken to Panama City. The rest belonged to his wife. As usual, he had not enjoyed himself. Two days of inactivity was his limit, but Terri, his wife, had insisted that he call in for an extra vacation day.

In the kitchen, he sorted through the accumulated mail his sister-in-law had brought in while they were gone. Finding nothing but bills, he took the stack of newspapers into the living room and sat down to look through them. The first, dated forty-eight hours after he had left for Florida, brought him to a state of hyperactivity. Sammy Turpin had been born excited; some things just made him more excited than others.

Terri entered the room, naked and carrying a towel. These trips always supercharged her libido, and she was hoping for a grand finale that evening. Sammy only glanced at her, however. She might as well have been wearing flannel. He was headed for the telephone.

"Who are you calling?" she asked sharply. Like the wives of all good cops, she knew how fast a husband could be lost to police work.

"Dispatch. There was a murder after we left"

"So what? You don't work homicide. Come on! Let's take a shower and go to bed."

"You don't understand. I think I was watching when this went down. It may have *happened* while I was watching!"

"Sammy, it's two in the morning! This can wait!" She saw her romantic interlude going down the drain.

"No, it can't wait. A homicide has less likelihood of being solved every day that it waits. Hello, this is Sammy Turpin. Lemme speak to Doyle Griffin or Gary Keith. . . . Oh all right, I'll call them at home."

"Sammy, they're gonna be pissed if you wake them up."

"Naw." He was flipping through his small book of phone numbers. Finding Griffin's number first, he dialed quickly.

"Sammy, we're still on vacation. Hang up the phone and come on."

"Doyle? This is Sammy Turpin. Listen, I think I may have watched this torso homicide go down the other night, just before I went to Panama City. I think it happened at the Devil's Son's clubhouse. I—" He was suddenly silent.

"All right, Doyle. Sorry. I'll get with you in the morning. Damn," Turpin said, "what a hothead! He's usually friendly."

"What did he say?" Terri asked smugly.

"He said the sonofabitch will still be dead tomorrow when he's back in his office."

"I told you. Let's take a shower and go to bed."

"I must have caught him at a bad time. I'll call Gary Keith."

"*Sammy!*"

"All right, I'll wait until morning," the chunky little intelligence officer said, "but if it was *my* case, I'd get up and work on it."

You would, too! she thought to herself.

Doyle Griffin was irritated as he entered the cramped office, a cigarette dangling from his mouth and a cup of black coffee in his hand. Gary Keith was already at his desk. Griffin grudgingly admitted that the new homicide investigator did not shirk his job.

"Anything new, Gary?"

"Matter of fact, yes. We now have almost all the body parts.

A couple exercising their poodle found a bag hung in the bushes at Choctaw Park, below the boat launch. I decided there was no reason for both of us to lose sleep."

"I appreciate that—even though Sammy Turpin woke me up, ranting and raving at two o'clock. What was in the bag?"

"Let's just say, we now have almost everything, except for the heart, the liver, and miscellaneous."

"The hands and arms? Good, if the fingerprints can be lifted after all this time—" Griffin said, putting out one cigarette and lighting another.

"Nope," Keith interrupted, sipping at a diet lemon-lime drink, "each and every finger-tip was snipped off. No help at all."

"Damn! We may never identify this son of a bitch."

"Look here." The investigator tossed several Polaroid pictures on the desk.

Griffin picked them up, sipping his coffee, and looked closely. "Is that what I think it is? Looks like a snake."

"Precisely what the woman who found it said. Real sophisticated lady and husband, but they didn't describe it any differently than you just did."

"Well, at least any woman who was intimate with him will be able to identify *that*." Griffin shook his head.

"I should think so," Keith laughed, reaching for the phone. "Homicide, Keith. . . . Does he look like a crazy? . . . Then send him back." He hung up the phone.

"They've got a guy in a three-piece suit out front. He says he may have information on our Jigsaw Man."

"Don't say that word, Gary."

"May as well," he shrugged. "Everyone else is."

The man knocked lightly on the door. He was about thirty-five, tall and well groomed. The suit he was wearing had not been bought off the rack. The briefcase he carried had come from a real cow. There was nothing plastic about the man.

"Come in and have a seat. I'm Sergeant Griffin. This is Investigator Keith. What can we do for you?"

"Well, I should have been here days ago, but you know

how it is. I just didn't want to get involved. But after I read what the medical examiner said, I decided I'd have to come in."

He opened the briefcase. They leaned over with interest as he removed a .22 caliber target pistol in a plastic bag and put it on Keith's desk.

"Maybe you'd better explain, Mr. . . ." Griffin began.

"Lloyd Carter. I bought this pistol a couple of weeks ago, but didn't get around to trying it out until the evening before you found the torso at the quarry."

"Go on, Mr. Carter," Keith said, looking directly into the man's eyes.

"I was plinking at cans, but I also fired three rounds into a silver garbage bag. I think that may account for the rounds in your torso. I might have let it go, but I knew it was important when I read what the doctor said about the cause of death."

The two officers looked at each other.

"We appreciate this, Mr. Carter," Griffin said. "We'll need for you to make a formal statement, and we'll have to send the pistol to ballistics."

"Of course, I understand. I'm just relieved that I've told you. What's the penalty for what I've done?"

"No penalty for firing a weapon in the county, Mr. Carter. If you'll follow me, I'll take you around to the secretary so you can get your statement on paper," Keith said.

When Keith returned, the silver-haired detective was sipping his coffee, cigarette in hand. "Close the door, Gary."

The investigator turned, a big smile on his face. "Do you know what that medical examiner is going to look like?"

"Matter of fact, I was just sittin' here savorin' that thought."

Suddenly, they both were laughing uncontrollably, releasing built-up tension from three days of frustration. When the laughter subsided, they wiped away the tears, divided up the best leads, and left the office to check them out.

Doyle had forgotten about Sammy Turpin, who was very upset when he arrived to find them both gone.

*   *   *

Keith pulled up in front of Hartford Towers. The building, a government-subsidized apartment complex for the elderly and disabled, rose stark and colorless against the morning sky. The anonymous woman caller had said it was where the victim might have lived—at least, the man she thought was the victim.

Keith and Griffin had already checked over a hundred "possibilities," only to find that the missing persons had returned home, called, or, in one case, was a black man. Every lead had to be checked, though, until they came up with an identification.

Inside, the slender homicide investigator discovered that the apartment complex had the smell of an institution about it. It was permeated with odors of cheap food cooking—cabbage, beans, and turnip greens.

He opened the door marked "office" and found a slatternly woman sitting behind a metal desk, cigarette dangling from her lips. She was about fifty and had the harried look of a prison warden.

"I'm Investigator Gary Keith. Are you the person in charge?" he asked, flipping open his badge case.

"I'm supposed to be, but nobody's really in charge of a bunch of retards and old people. They don't listen."

They must have scoured the bottom of the barrel to find such a warm personality, Keith thought as he fished the notepad from his pocket. "I'm checking on a . . . Larry Foglesong."

"What's he done?" She shuffled a stack of papers on her desk.

"You know him, then?"

"Yeah, but it don't seem likely that he'd be in trouble with the police."

"I didn't say he was. Is he a tenant here?"

"You don't have to get snippy about it. He *was* a tenant here until about a month ago."

"Do you have a file on him? Maybe a forwarding address or information about his family?"

"Yeah, I got all that." She rose and went to a metal filing

cabinet. "You're barkin' up the wrong tree. He ain't real bright, not since he kissed the backend of a dump truck, but he ain't no criminal either. . . . Here it is. He moved to 2822 Tarbell Road. Moved in with a coupla former residents here— Eddie Courtney and Alma Thurber."

"What can you tell me about Larry Foglesong?"

"Well, he ain't exactly stupid. It's more like he's about fifteen years old. He went to trade school for a while, but it didn't last. He just couldn't get along with most people. All he was really interested in was tinkerin' with his old car and ridin' his motorcycle. I had to make him store the motorcycle somewhere else. He was always tunin' it up makin' a lot of noise."

"Was he violent?"

"Nothin' like that. Just childish." The woman pushed a strand of hair from her face. "Like in the TV room, if there was somethin' he wanted to watch, he'd pitch a fit to get it."

"What about these friends, Courtney and Thurber?"

"Eddie lived next door to him and Alma lived across the hall. They both was after Alma all the time. She played 'em off against each other."

"How old is Alma?" Keith asked.

"About forty-five. She had a stroke a few years ago. Can't hardly tell by lookin', but she's on Social Security."

"I thought Foglesong was in his late twenties."

"Oh, you mean the age difference? Honey, around here, a woman in her forties is a spring chicken."

"Why did they leave?"

"The older people got to complainin' about Larry and Eddie arguin' over Alma all the time. I'd had rent problems out of those two, so I told 'em to leave. A month later Larry moved out and went to live with 'em."

"What is Eddie Courtney's disability and age?"

"Middle thirties. Had a stroke, same as Alma. Almost as childish as Larry. Eddie's got a crippled arm from the stroke. Can't use it too much."

"Did you say you have a phone number or address for Foglesong's family?"

"Sure." The woman jotted down a name and address, then added a phone number. "His mother lives in Ohio. She came down and got him installed here. I doubt that she knows about him movin' out, considerin' how upset she was when she found out that he was livin' part-time with a girl once before."

"Do you know the girl's name?"

"Naw. Sherry somethin' or another. She had a couple of brats. That's all I knew about her."

"You've been very helpful." He handed her a business card. "Could you give me a call if Larry shows up?"

"Sure, honey. It ain't likely, though. Them retards all need each other."

"Mrs. Waters, I'm Sergeant Griffin from the sheriff's department. You talked to my partner, Investigator Keith, yesterday."

"Yes." She was hesitant. "Come in, Sergeant." She was a tired, worn woman in her early sixties.

Doyle entered the kitchen and looked around. It reminded him of his boyhood. The walls were papered with a floral design, and in the center of the room was a table with a checkered tablecloth.

"Can I get you a cup of coffee, Sergeant? I just fixed a pot."

"I'd appreciate that, Mrs. Waters." He accepted the coffee to put her at ease more than anything else, though the freshly perked coffee did smell good.

He took a sip before speaking to her. "My partner said you had some concerns to share with us?"

"I hope it's nothin', but I been worried. It's about my son."

"Tell me about it."

"The evenin' before the cut-up body was found, I carried out the garbage and found bloody clothes in the garbage can. I thought nothin' of it 'til he lied to me about it. There's all kinds of ways to get bloody on a farm. He said the clothes was ruint with grease."

"Did you save the clothes, Mrs. Waters?"

71

"I went to get 'em later, but John had already carried off the trash. He takes it to a county collection center once a week."

"Besides the clothes, what else has been botherin' you?"

"I found silver garbage bags under the sink. I never buy that kind—always black ones. There was several already missin' when I found 'em."

Doyle sipped his coffee, watching the woman. It was not hard for him to understand how an imagination could run rampant.

"Mrs. Waters, I understand your concern, but I'm sure these things are just coincidence."

"I'm worried about the workshop, too." She was twisting her apron between her hands. "I want you to look in there before you go. He keeps it locked, and I've never been in there."

"Mrs. Waters, I can't break into a locked room without probable cause. I'm sorry."

"He leaves his keyring here while he's in the fields. It's *my* house and *my* barn."

"Well, in that case, to put your mind at ease, let's go have a look."

He waited quietly as she went after the keys. There were places he needed to go, but he felt sorry for the elderly woman. It would only take a few minutes to give her peace of mind.

It was a good barn, Doyle noticed with the appreciative eye of a country boy. It was neat, everything in its place.

The woman turned the key in the large padlock, removed it, took a deep breath, and pushed it open. Seeing that she was reluctant to enter, Doyle felt around for the light switch and flipped it on.

His eyes narrowed as he took in the scene.

In the center of the room was a gleaming stainless steel table. Across the back of the room were meathooks on a wire. The thing that caught his eye, though, was the rack of gleaming knives.

Tile had been laid on the floor. There was a brass drain in

the center and a double aluminum sink against the wall. The entire place sparkled.

"Mrs. Waters, does your son butcher his own livestock?"

"One beef and a pig. That's all. We don't need *this* for what we use."

"This looks like a professional outfit, Mrs. Waters."

"Sergeant, there's more about John that I didn't mention."

"What's that?"

"In the navy, John was trained as a meat-cutter . . . and his girlfriend Sarah . . . I think she's a witch."

"I can't believe Doyle didn't even mention that I called last night." Sammy Turpin stalked around the room in his normal hyperactive state. "I've been here *two* hours."

"He did mention it, Sammy. We just had a lot to do," Keith said, putting his notebook on the desk.

"I may have watched the fight that ended in the murder," Turpin informed him.

"Tell me about it." Keith opened the small refrigerator and took out a diet soda. "You want something to drink?"

"No. The night before I left for Florida, I had the Devil's Sons staked out. There was a fight between Bonzo Carlin and a big, blond guy. I didn't see how it ended, because they fell into the kitchen. The guy fit the description of the murder victim. An hour or so later, they carried out some garbage bags and loaded them on a pickup."

"Silver bags?" Keith watched the criminal intelligence officer with narrowed eyes.

"I couldn't tell. It was too dark."

"An hour wouldn't be much time to butcher a body, Sammy."

"It'd be plenty of time with three guys workin' on it."

"I'll get to this as soon as I can, Sammy."

"You don't believe me, do you?" Turpin asked angrily.

"Yes, I believe you, but I also know that you let your feelings about the bikers get out of hand sometimes."

"You're all alike! You think my job is a joke, except for

David Lark. He's the only one who keeps up with them. He filled out two field interrogation cards while I was gone. Nobody else is interested, though." Turpin threw the cards on the desk in disgust.

"It's not that we don't take you seriously, Sammy." Keith picked up the cards to placate the chunky little investigator. "But you do get obsessed with them." He started to put the cards down, when something caught his eye.

"When did Lark stop this pickup?"

"Day before yesterday, why?"

"Maybe nothing, but I was just getting ready to make a call about one of the names on this card. The bikers had a motorcycle belonging to Larry Foglesong on the back of the pickup."

"Foglesong? Yeah, that tag has turned up at the clubhouse and around biker bars a few times. He's not a biker, though. I don't know him."

"Sammy, let me make a call to Ohio. We may need to take a *very* close look at the clubhouse."

John Waters watched from a clump of trees as the tall, silver-haired detective carried a bag from the barn to his cruiser. They *knew*, or they would soon know.

He had almost walked right up on them before he noticed the police car. His own mother had turned him in! It should have come as no surprise. She had watched the old man abuse him for seventeen years—until he had finally run away to join the navy.

God! What am I going to do? Where can I go? he agonized.

One thing was certain. He could not be locked up. The very thought smothered him. The childhood memory of the stifling basement was as real as it had ever been.

It would be hard to prove. His fanaticism about cleanliness would make it difficult for them. They would *know*, but it would take a while for them to put it together. Everything in that workshop, from knives to floor, had been meticulously scrubbed with ammonia, leaving no trace of blood. It was only a matter of time, though.

*   *   *

"Mrs. Foglesong?"

"Yes," a pleasant voice said from the other end of the line, "may I help you?"

"This is Investigator Gary Keith from Horton, Tennessee. I need to ask you a couple of questions."

"It's about Larry, isn't it?" The concern was real, but there was also a tone of resignation.

"I honestly don't know, Mrs. Foglesong. Are you there alone? If you are, I'd like for you to get with another family member and call me back."

"Officer, my daughter is here, but I have survived the death of a husband and two stillborn infants without going to pieces. Don't keep me in suspense. Ask your questions."

"Could you give me a physical description of Larry?"

"He's five-eleven and weighs about two-twenty. He's blond, wears his hair about shoulder length, and usually a mustache. You can't tell by looking, but he had serious head injuries in a motorcycle accident several years ago."

"Any tattoos or other scars?"

"Not that I know of. Officer, Larry was in junior college when the accident happened; a bright, normal young man. After the accident, he was never quite the same. We sent him down there to stay with an aunt because it depressed him so much to be around people who knew him before. When his aunt died, he chose to stay. Has something happened to my son?"

"Mrs. Foglesong, is there *any* type of outstanding physical attribute—a mole, perhaps—that your son had?"

"Officer, I don't know how to say this delicately, but my son was always . . . well, he was sexually well endowed. So much so, that other boys used to make fun of him."

"Mrs. Foglesong, is there a dentist there who has worked on Larry's teeth?"

"Yes. I'll call and have him mail the charts."

"If you don't mind, just have him call the Horton County coroner's office and read the chart to them."

"So you think my son is a murder victim?" Her voice barely trembled.

"Yes ma'am, from what you just told me, I do. I'll confirm it after the dental chart is called in."

"I'll be there tomorrow."

"If you'll wait, I'll call you back and verify," Keith said.

"All right," she agreed. "I want to know as soon as you hear from the dentist."

Keith hung up the phone and turned to Turpin. "Get me a report on what you saw, Sammy. I'll see if we have enough for a search warrant for the Devil's Sons' clubhouse. It looks like Foglesong is our Jigsaw Man."

The phone rang before Turpin could say anything. "Keith, Homicide."

"This is Bill Chalmers at the F.B.I. office. The lab raised the printing on the suitcase tag you sent. The name is Larry Foglesong."

"Thanks. I'll have someone pick up the report."

Keith hung up the phone and sat staring at the wall. It had already been a long day—and it was Halloween.

Neither he nor his partner had been listening to the radio or watching television. If they had, they would have heard all about the "world famous psychic," Samantha Thorpe, who had come to Horton to assist the police in finding the jigsaw murderer. She was holding a psychic work session that evening at a local occult bookstore.

The media, lacking real news because the police were reluctant to discuss the case, planned to make a big event of it.

Chapter Nine

Eighteen sheriff's deputies sat waiting for roll call to start. They had just been briefed by Investigator Gary Keith of the latest findings about the "so-called" jigsaw murder case. Keith had brought along some interesting pictures that he had shown them with an admonition that none of the information be discussed with outsiders.

"You guys can call him the Jigsaw Man, if you want," Patrol Officer Jenny Tharp said, "but after seeing those pictures, *I'm* gonna call him 'King.' I'd tip my hat in respect, if I hadn't left it in the car."

"I think it's all a lot of hullabaloo over nothin'," Jumbo Patterson replied. "Size don't mean anything. It's the skill of the magician, not the size of the wand that matters. I can tell you right now, if he had any more fun with that one than I have with mine, he'd have died of pleasure."

Jenny Tharp turned in her front row seat to look at Jumbo. A Spanish-looking woman of dark coloration, she was lean and of medium height with hair falling to her shoulders in violation of departmental rules which said it should be kept up. She smiled sweetly.

"Jumbo, the truth is, whether or not *you* have fun is of secondary concern to your partner. Ask *her* whether she prefers a little one like yours or the king-sized variety."

"The subject never came up before, Jenny. It happens that I am a skilled magician," the big, blond officer said smugly.

"Most of you *have* to be magicians to get results with those *teeny-weeny* little wands you carry!"

The room was filled with catcalls, whistles, and bravos. There was twenty seconds of clapping for Jenny as Jumbo slid down in his chair, cheeks flaming.

"*You* don't have any firsthand knowledge of the size of my equipment," Jumbo hissed to Jenny.

"That's right, Jumbo, I don't. I just took your girlfriend's word when she said 'Jumbo' refers to your imagination."

This time, Jenny stood for the applause as Jumbo sat sullenly in his chair, thinking of pay-back. He was finished for the afternoon, though. Enough was enough.

For once, Jumbo was glad to see Sergeant Vince Jordan come in for roll call. A man of medium height and build, Jordan's uniforms always had knife-edge creases because he never did anything strenuous enough to muss them. The captain and lieutenant were both on days off, which happened twice a month. Sergeant Jordan made the most of those two days.

It was an established fact that Vince Jordan could supervise more in two days than anyone else could supervise in a month. Before coming to Alpha Detachment, he had been on Charlie Detachment. The commander there, Captain Jergen, had demanded that Jordan be transferred because the sergeant had almost supervised the detachment into a mutiny, stemming from an insistence that the officers spend 80 percent of their time writing citations.

"All right, listen up," Jordan said, putting his hat on the lectern. He was the only officer on the detachment who wore his hat to roll call, or at any other time for that matter, though it was departmental policy.

Jordan brought the same high priorities that had endeared him to his former subordinates in Alpha Detachment: writing tickets, wearing a hat, and making Sergeant Vince Jordan look good.

"Tonight is Halloween—" Jordan began.

"No shit!" Jenny Tharp muttered incredulously to the patrol officer next to her. "Tonight's *Halloween?* Did you know that?"

"I didn't know it," he answered. "Did you know it, Midget?"

"No, but I'm sure glad the sergeant brought it up. Can you imagine what we would have *thought* when we saw all the little goblins tonight?"

Jordan stood, a stony expression on his face, until the joke made its way around the squad room. He would have written letters of reprimand for insubordination, but he knew the captain would never let them get past his desk. On Jordan's first day on the shift, he had asked the captain for permission to ride one night with each patrol officer.

"Why? We're short of cars now," the captain had asked.

"To show them what to look for. You know, give them little pointers as they make the rounds."

"Tell you what," the captain answered, going back to his paperwork. "If I ever get a patrol officer who knows less than you, I'll let you ride with him."

Letters of reprimand being out of the question, Jordan did his best to ignore the sniping remarks of the jealous (he was certain that was why they disliked him) officers, most of whom had only high school diplomas.

"If you people are finished with your childish attempts at humor, I'll continue." He paused, enormous Prussian mustache quivering with contempt, and waited for silence. Vince had always planned on being a captain by the age of thirty. At thirty-three, he found himself blocked by cops who insisted on following only supervisors for whom they had respect.

"I'll be running two cars wild tonight—in light of the special holiday. Tharp, you cover the northwest. Patterson, you cover the southeast.

"Last evening," he broke out his little notebook, "I saw six officers out of the car without hats—"

"Did you see any officer *with* a hat?" Midget asked.

"I'm tired of warning you people," he continued, ignoring Midget's question. "The administration has seen fit to write these dress code regulations, and I intend for this detachment to abide by them.

"Homicide has briefed you on the latest information about the torso killing. No doubt we will be receiving calls relating to garbage bags all evening. I would appreciate it if you would answer those calls without provoking a near riot such as we had over the chicken entrails.

"We ended up putting four people in jail last shift. That time could have been better spent—"

"Writin' traffic citations, maybe?" Jumbo interrupted.

"Yes, for *one* thing! This detachment is sadly lacking in its enthusiasm for traffic enforcement!" Jordan snapped.

"That's because we didn't sign on to be meter maids," Jenny Tharp retorted.

This brought a fresh infusion of blood to the sergeant's face. He had headed the now-defunct traffic division. It had been his pride and joy, but it had lasted only five months before being dismantled as ineffective.

Jordan stood glaring at the woman officer, who only smiled back benignly. It was the same smile she had given him the day he asked her out. She had thanked him for thinking of her, but said she didn't go out with assholes.

"Weapons check," Jordan said, changing the subject. There had been an inspection the day before, but Jordan suspected that the lieutenant always tipped them off so he would not discover unauthorized ammunition suitable for killing elephants in their weapons.

"I got mine," Jumbo said, holding his weapon in the air. "Have you got yours, Midget?"

"Yeah, I got mine. Have you got yours, Jenny?"

"Never mind! Move out!" Jordan yelled, as the entire detachment began to wave revolvers in the air.

"Damn, I wonder what upset the sergeant?" Jumbo asked as they were filing out.

"I have no idea," Jenny Tharp answered, "unless the pansy is having his period this week."

*   *   *

Jordan went back into the supervisor's office and sat down, near tears in frustration. He had been voted most likely to succeed by his graduating class at East Tennessee State University. He was a certified accident reconstructionist with more impressive credentials than anyone else in the department. Why could he not command respect?

With a sigh, he picked up his radio. "Alpha 3," he said.

"Go ahead, Alpha 3," the dispatcher replied.

"Alpha Detachment is clear for service."

"10–4, Alpha 3. All other units: Alpha Detachment is now clear for service."

At least the dispatchers are properly respectful, Jordan said to himself, unaware of the conversation taking place in the communications office.

"Well, we can all relax," said one plump, blonde dispatcher with curly ringlets. "The *mobile dispatcher* is now in the field."

"Yeah," an older woman said, "what an asshole!"

Chapter Ten

It began to get dark at seven-thirty. By nine o'clock the Horton police department and the sheriff's department had received over a hundred "silver garbage bags calls." The officers had found bags containing everything from cow manure to ordinary garbage along side roads, inside storage sheds, and in fields and ditches.

The little goblins were having the time of their lives watching cops run their behinds off.

Midget Poplin and Jumbo Patterson stopped as they met each other coming in opposite directions. There had been several complaints of youths in a silver Mercedes hurling bags of blood against the fronts of houses. The bags were not silver, but they were messy. Outraged parents whose children were out vandalizing other people's homes indignantly demanded action.

"You believe this, Midget? Vandals in a Mercedes Benz?"

"You just ain't worked the west end enough, Jumbo. These rich kids destroy more property than the slum kids. It just gets fixed down here. Almost every one of these little snots has a street sign on his wall. They replace some of them four or five times a year. You catch 'em, and the parents buy their way out. Boys will be boys, you know."

"I thought a silver Mercedes would be easy to find. I've seen four already."

"That's the way it is down here," Midget replied philosophically.

"Hey!" Jumbo was looking at the intersection behind Midget. "A silver Mercedes just busted that stop sign." He hit his blue lights, tires squealing. Midget backed into a driveway and followed. A minute later, Jumbo was calling in a tag number. Midget pulled in behind Jumbo and walked to the passenger side. Inside the car were four boys approximately sixteen to eighteen years old.

"Is that a box of garbage bags I see in the back seat?" Jumbo asked.

"Yeah," the driver said. "We're collecting aluminum cans for a school fund-raising drive." He was blond with curly hair. His cheeks were spotted with a stubborn case of acne that even the most expensive dermatologists could not cure. He looked at his friends and giggled.

Slowly the gargantuan officer leaned down until his face was level with the boy's, his eyebrows rolled together like thunderheads. Jumbo Patterson was a man who could intimidate old-time barroom brawlers. The boy swallowed hard.

"I hate a smartass punk." Jumbo clipped off each word.

"He can't talk to you like that, Tip," a chunky boy with spiked hair said from the back seat. He recoiled from Jumbo's glance and said nothing else.

"Get out of the car, Tip," Jumbo said quietly, "and bring your keys. The rest of you break out some identification and hand it to that other officer."

The slender youth got out of the car nervously. The officer stood looking at him without speaking for almost thirty seconds.

"Now, Tip, I am going to very courteously ask you to walk back and open the trunk. I don't expect any mouth from you."

"You don't have to do nothing he says!" The boy with the spiked hair seemed to be regaining his courage.

"Yeah . . . uh, my dad's a lawyer. He won't like it if you violate my rights!" The boy tried to bluster but did not quite pull it off.

"Tip, I'm not gonna hold it against you because your

daddy's a maggot. Now, once more nicely. *Please* open the trunk."

The boy walked back and reluctantly raised the lid. There were three ten-gallon plastic paint buckets. Newspapers had been laid out on the bottom of the trunk. The officer reached in and popped the lid off one of the buckets. It was half-full of partially congealed blood. The other two buckets were full.

"Where'd you get the blood, Tip?"

"I bought it at a slaughterhouse yesterday. It's pig blood. It ain't against the law, is it?" The boy was trembling, but trying to become defiant again.

"To possess blood? Of course not. Vandalism, now that's another matter. Some of these people who are spending their valuable time cleaning blood off their houses might be happy to prosecute."

"That's a joke. I know the law. You can't convict somebody of a crime unless you can *identify* them." Seventeen years of pampered protection was restoring his confidence in Daddy's ability to get him out of anything.

"So what you're sayin', Tip, is that nobody got a close enough look at you to identify you?"

"I'm saying that my daddy'll make you look like a fool if you try to charge me."

"Well, I wouldn't want that to happen, Tip. Why don't you go get back in the car. I'll close the trunk."

The boy's face was a picture of adolescent triumph as he took his seat behind the wheel. His father was right. Cops are a bunch of blowhards. "Hurry up and shut that trunk," he yelled over his shoulder, "we ain't got all night."

Midget was about to say something, as he handed identification back to the other three, when Jumbo winked at him. The big officer was taking his time closing the trunk.

"Sorry, Tip, I was just putting the lids back on."

"In that case, I might not tell my dad how rude you were," the pimply rich kid said. He pulled away and turned down the hill. He was going to enjoy telling his friends how he had backed down the big, ignorant cop.

"I hope there was some reason for letting that little bastard talk to you like that," Midget said.

"He's going downhill," Jumbo smiled, "and there's a stop sign. When he puts on his brakes, twenty-five gallons of pig blood, no longer in the containers, is gonna pour from the trunk into the passenger compartment. Tip's a smart kid. I think he'll figure out who had the last word, don't you?"

They both burst out laughing and shook hands. The case of the silver Mercedes was closed, a simple case handled in curbstone court.

"Hurry up, Doyle," Gary Keith called out. "They're about to interview her."

Doyle Griffin sauntered into the squadroom where his partner had set up a small black and white television set scrounged from the property room. The perpetual cigarette dangled from his mouth, and a cup of coffee completed the image.

"I still can't believe they're actually gonna interview her," Doyle muttered, looking for an ashtray.

"It's Halloween," Keith explained. "Last year this station went to a séance. It's just a gimmick." He poured a cup of his usual diet lemon-lime soda and sat back.

"Yeah, and it's gonna cause the phone to ring five hundred times tonight. I guarantee it."

"Quiet. Here it is."

"Welcome to 'Focus,' a local program of local interest. Tonight we will interview Samantha Thorpe, a psychic of national fame. Less than two days ago, while being interviewed on a talk show in Asheville, Samantha collapsed and went into what she has described as a trance. During that trance she claimed to have made a psychic connection with a murder in this city, a brutal murder, now being called the case of the Jigsaw Man . . ."

"Damn! There's that word again," Doyle growled.

The television hostess, a wholesome girl who would have been at ease in the line of a high-school cheerleading squad, stood outside the New Age, an occult bookstore. It was a run-down, brick building with graffiti on the walls.

The camera followed her through the door, past esoteric objects behind glass and on shelves. Part of the store owner's agreement to let them film there had been for a quick pan of his stock.

"In here," the hostess said dramatically, "Samantha Thorpe has spent the afternoon meditating in a darkened room. She will share with us her experience—and hopefully help us along in the investigation of one of Horton's most brutal murders."

Samantha sat, long, raven-colored hair falling over her left shoulder. The semidarkened room suited her well. Not only did it lend an air of mystery, but it also made it easier to hide the sagging chin, which no longer was as firm and smooth as it had been when Samantha's hairstyle was popular.

"She looks like a witch in a Hollywood horror film," Doyle exclaimed. "But you know, her appearance matches her voice."

"How do you know? She hasn't said anything yet."

"She called this afternoon," Doyle answered, lighting a fresh cigarette.

"And you didn't tell *me?*" Keith asked, not believing what he had just heard. His high forehead climbed higher when he was enraged.

"I knew you'd talk to her, because you're polite. I didn't want to give her any quotations. I just told her we'd solve our own case and hung up."

"You know, Doyle, it's just *possible* that some psychics are real. She might have been able to help us."

"Nope. They're all fakes. You'll see that when we solve this case with old-fashioned police work. Listen, she's on."

". . . and as I said before, I had never had any contact with Horton before that night. I suppose the psychic vibrations were so strong that night that they affected me all the way over in Asheville." Samantha tossed the mane of hair.

"Have you been in contact with the Horton County Sheriff's Department since your arrival, Samantha?" The blonde, young reporter leaned forward with the microphone.

"Yes, I have. Unfortunately, as in so many instances, police officers feel threatened by my presence. They fear it will reflect on their abilities."

"Bull," Doyle Griffin muttered.

"Let's *listen!* All right? I want to hear what she has to say. An investigator should never close his mind to *anything.*"

Doyle decided the young investigator was definitely upset.

The light of the television cast pale shadows around the room. The statue of Pan sparkled as the two-faced god Janus laughed and cried at opposite walls.

"Tell us your perceptions, Samantha. What have you learned?"

"The killer is a sophisticated, highly intelligent individual. I saw a man with a high forehead, and perhaps glasses. I think he's probably an artist of some kind, the leader of a group that practices the black arts. The Jigsaw Man was a pre-Halloween sacrifice. He directed the dismemberment, but others carried it out."

"Pre-Halloween, Samantha? Are you saying that there may be another killing tonight?" the reporter asked breathlessly.

"That's entirely possible," Samantha answered, shaking her mane of black hair.

All over Horton County, parents rushed to their cars to retrieve little ghosts and goblins, seeing visions of their children stretched out like sacrificial lambs.

"Liar."

"What?" John Waters asked drowsily. It had taken two sleeping pills to calm him down after he had arrived nearly hysterical, having seen the detective leave his "workshop."

"Liar. She's a phony," Sarah repeated, getting out of bed. Walking to the television, she changed to a channel where cartoons were being shown.

"How do you know?" he asked drowsily, almost able to believe that everything would be all right.

"Because I can *tell*, that's why. The woman has no aura around her." Sarah walked across the room to the center of the circle on the floor. She leaned over, the light reflecting off her buttocks, and lit a block of incense.

"What are you doin'?"

"I'm getting ready. This is a sacred night. I'll raise a cone of power to protect you," she said, standing up to look at him.

"You can't protect me," he slurred his words. "They found my workshop. He has some of my tools. They'll *know* what I did in there. I cleaned the tools, but they'll *know*."

"I can protect you," she said. "My magic is strong. Supper is almost ready. I've baked a nice meat pie. You'll feel better after you eat. Then we'll raise the cone of power and call on the old gods."

"What kind of meat pie?" he asked in a voice like a child.

"Liver, heart, and sweetbreads," she answered with a smile, the light from the television reflecting softly off her crimson lips and white teeth. "*Strong* magic."

"Do I have to eat it?"

"Yes, baby. You have to eat it. Sarah knows what's good for you."

Chapter Eleven

"This is the place," Gary Keith said. "Twenty-eight, twenty-two Tarbell."

Griffin and he had ridden in strained silence to the rural community. The young investigator was still angry at Griffin for his treatment of the psychic the previous day. It was not that Keith believed in psychics, but it was *his* case. Griffin had no business making that kind of decision.

"Heard from the Ohio dentist yet?" Griffin asked.

"No. The mother called back. She was having trouble locating him. As soon as we get confirmation, the judge will sign a search warrant on the Devil's Sons' clubhouse."

"That's a possibility, I guess," Griffin said, flipping his cigarette out the passenger side window.

"You don't think it was bikers?"

"It's possible. I still wanna talk to John Waters, though, and his girlfriend, the witch. His mother called last night. He didn't come home. I've got an address to check this afternoon. I wanna know why the man has a butcher shop in his barn. They don't even raise cattle."

"Maybe Waters is connected to the bikers some way. The farm isn't very far from Holbert's Quarry," Keith suggested. "Look, the curtain moved up there in the kitchen. Let's go talk to Foglesong's roommates."

The house was run down, the white paint flaking from the old weatherboard covering. Once a gay red color, the porch was now a lifeless gray. It shook as they walked across it. Keith rapped on the door.

A moment later, the door opened a crack, revealing half a face surrounded by brittle brown hair. "Whatcha want?" a female voice asked.

"Police officers," Keith said, holding up his badge case. "Are you Alma Thurber?"

"Yeah. What's wrong?"

"We just need to ask you and Eddie Courtney a few questions. Is he here?"

"It's about the car, ain't it?" She opened the door with resignation. "I told Eddie we shouldn't drive the car."

"What car?" Keith asked, glancing at the sergeant.

"We had an accident in Larry's car the other night." She stepped out of the way and let them in.

The woman was wearing colorless slacks and a man's shirt. Knowing her to be forty-five, Keith decided that she looked every day of it, and he wondered why two men would ever have argued over her. With a slight limp, the result of a stroke, he remembered, she led the way inside.

The kitchen was what Griffin had expected. The floor was covered with cheap linoleum, broken in places. The wall was painted a sick pink color, in jarring contrast with the plastic counter of garish yellow floral design. The place smelled of cooked cabbage.

"The cops have come to talk to us about wreckin' Larry's car," she said to the man who rose from in front of the television as they entered. She sounded almost triumphant.

"It ain't against the law to drive a car if the owner leaves it with you! Is it?" The man looked imploringly at the officers. His left arm hung limply at his side. He was of medium build, with dark thinning hair. His eyes had terror in them.

"Look," Keith said, "there's been a misunderstanding. We just need to ask some questions about Larry Foglesong. Something may have happened to him. What's this about a car?"

"You ain't here about the wreck?" The woman seemed amazed.

"What wreck?" Doyle Griffin asked quietly.

"We took Larry's car to the grocery store and had a little accident," the man answered. "It wasn't anything."

"Why doesn't Larry have his car with him?"

"He was goin' to pick up his motorcycle, then come back for his car later," the man said. "He got mad and moved out. The car is in the shed out back—hardly hurt at all."

"Where was his motorcycle?" Keith asked.

"Them bikers he hung around with had it," the man said. "They was supposed to have it fixed. It throwed a rod."

"Did Larry hang around the bikers a lot?"

"Yeah," the woman replied. "They're mean people. They made fun of Larry and spent his Social Security money, but he always thought they was his friends."

"May we sit down?" Keith asked.

"Sure," the woman replied. "Would y'all like some coffee?"

"No, thanks. When did you see Larry last?"

"It was a week ago, yesterday," the man answered. "What's happened to Larry?"

"Maybe nothing. You said he got mad and left. What was he mad about?"

Before the man could answer, Doyle's radio crackled, calling for either Keith or Griffin. The sergeant responded and was told to call the dispatcher.

"Do you have a phone I can use?" Griffin asked.

"Right there in the bedroom," the woman nodded her head.

"Go ahead, Mr. Courtney," Keith told him.

"It was because of Alma," the man dropped his eyes. "He was always makin' indecent proposals to her and sneakin' looks at her while she was nekkid in the bathroom."

"Were you ever intimate with Larry Foglesong, Alma?"

"What?"

"He means, did you ever let him do it to you?" Eddie Courtney said.

"No," she modestly dropped her eyes. "He was too young

91

for me—just twenty-nine. I'm ten years older." Gary did not bother to tell her that he knew her true age.

"What about you two? Are you lovers?"

"What's it to you?" Courtney's pale blue eyes lit up with fire for a moment.

"He's got to ask questions, Eddie. No. You see . . . well, Eddie can't do it, on account of his stroke."

"It's only temporary! It'll come back!" Eddie Courtney insisted.

"That's all right, Mr. Courtney," Keith said soothingly. "Tell me about how Larry left."

"Well, I caught him lookin' through the door at Alma again. We had an argument, and he packed his stuff in that old brown suitcase of his and left carryin' it. He called somebody before he left. He said they'd pick him up on the road and take him to get his motorcycle."

"Eddie, I understand that you and Alma left Hartford Towers because you and Larry were arguing over Alma. How is it you let him move in?"

"Well, he promised to do better . . . and it's hard to live on our pensions—"

"And Larry had a car," Alma Thurber chimed in. The man glared at her as she brought up the subject of the car again.

"Gary," Griffin interrupted, coming from the bedroom, "we need to go get that search warrant. The dentist just called from Ohio. Alma, Eddie, I hate to be the one to tell you this, but your friend Larry is dead."

The woman gasped and covered her face. Eddie Courtney stared at them as if stunned.

"We'll have the car towed in for processing," Keith said. "Don't touch it until someone arrives." The two officers left quickly.

"If you'd a kept your mouth shut," the man said harshly, after the door closed, "we coulda kept the car!" The woman did not reply, but her mouth set in a harsh line.

Outside, Gary Keith started the cruiser. "Can you imagine trying to get a look at *her* naked body?"

"A man'd have to be desperate, wouldn't he?" Griffin chuckled, easing the tension that had been between them.

"Well, if that psychic was right, we don't need to put Courtney on the list of suspects," Keith said.

"How's that?" Griffin lit a cigarette.

"She said the killer is a highly intelligent man. Courtney's I.Q. is about room temperature—in a cold house."

They both laughed, heading into the City-County Building to have a judge sign a search warrant for the Devil's Sons' clubhouse.

"By the way," Griffin remembered. "Records found an accident report. The clerk said to tell you that Foglesong's car was being driven by Eddie Courtney night before last."

"Everybody really comes through with information, *after* you get it somewhere else," Keith sighed.

"That's the way it usually goes," Griffin drawled, lighting a cigarette.

The door to the Devil's Sons' clubhouse opened as Doyle Griffin, Sammy Turpin, and Gary Keith entered the gate in the eight-foot wooden fence. Like all clubhouses run by the club, it was laid out like a fortress, and an alarm had sounded inside as they opened the gate.

The three detectives walked rapidly up the steps, followed by two husky sheriff's patrol officers. Four officers from the Horton city police sprinted in behind them and fanned out to surround the house. Two were carrying pump shotguns.

"Whatta you want?" the stringy-haired man asked from inside. He was a prospect, assigned to all the petty jobs around the clubhouse, such as guard duty.

"We have a search warrant," Griffin answered without breaking stride. The man attempted to shut the door, but Griffin's foot slammed against it, knocking him backwards.

"Cops!" the prospect yelled at the top of his lungs. Upstairs, feet loudly hit the floor.

Sprinting up the stairs, Gary Keith and Sammy Turpin met a naked woman as she threw open a door at the head of the steps. Behind her a man with reddish hair and the long biker beard jerked open a window, looking over his shoulder.

"It's Bonzo!" Turpin yelled, trying to get around the naked woman blocking their progress.

As the officers pushed past the determined woman, the biker climbed onto the window sill and hurled himself out the window. Grabbing a tree limb, he swung to the roof of a shed on the other side of the wooden fence. The two city patrol officers began to look frantically for a rear gate, but there was none.

Seeing his prime suspect escaping, Keith climbed to the window sill.

"Don't do it, Gary. You'll break your neck!" Turpin yelled.

Looking down, Keith swallowed hard. As the biker slid noisily off the tin roof of the shed, sending dry leaves and dust flying, the homicide officer leaped, catching the tree limb. For a moment he swung erratically, then hurled himself to the roof of the shed. He slid down the sloped roof, ripping a new jacket and scraping his hand.

When he hit the ground running, about thirty yards behind the biker, he noticed Bonzo was wearing no shoes. All he had to do was stay with him until the pain forced a halt. Keith, a non-smoker, decided he could do that.

The biker, however, was under an adrenaline rush, totally unaware of the pain in his feet as the jagged rocks cut into them. He ran like a deer, gaining distance on the cop behind him. Turning abruptly, he ran across a backyard through a child's play area.

Looking ahead, Keith did not see the small bicycle before he ran into it, going head over heels, arms and legs flying, and smashing his face into the soft ground. Turning to look back at the sound of the officer crashing, Bonzo ran full speed into the wire fence surrounding the house. Bouncing back, he fell full length.

Keith raised up and looked directly into the biker's face. They were separated by about fifty feet. The biker had hooded, blue eyes. His breath was coming in spurts. He had the look of an Old Testament prophet as he lay there.

"Why are you chasin' me?" Bonzo gasped.

"Why are you running?"

"Because you're chasin' me."

"I chased you because you ran."

"Well, I'm still runnin'!" He jumped to his feet and ran through a gate in the fence.

"Damn!" Keith muttered to himself, pushing up from the ground. In the world of TV police drama, the suspect would have been in custody by now, captured by a cordon of cops. Keith jogged along, wondering how the overweight biker was doing it.

Running through another yard, hair and beard streaming behind him, the biker almost stepped on a Doberman pinscher. The dog gave a yelp of fear, which turned to rage as Keith passed him. The dog was suddenly grabbing at his pants leg, tearing cloth every time he grabbed.

As Keith turned to kick at the ninety-pound dog, it grabbed him by the calf. Enraged, the officer drew his two-inch revolver. As he sighted in for a shot, the dog yelped and ran back the way it had come.

"I guess the dog understands attitudes perfectly," he grunted to himself as he turned and looked for Bonzo. Cursing under his breath, he limped back to the street knowing Bonzo would not be found that day. A city police cruiser pulled up.

"Damn if you ain't a mess," the big patrolman said. "Get in and I'll take you back to the clubhouse."

Limping on the injured leg, trousers and coat ripped, and with mud and grass on his face and hands, Keith got in the cruiser. "How come it never turns out like this in the movies?" he asked. The officer only shrugged.

Upon arrival at the clubhouse, Keith saw that the naked woman from upstairs (now clothed) was sitting in the back of a sheriff's department cruiser, staring angrily ahead.

Several assault rifles were spread out on the hood of a county cruiser as the patrolman checked with records for serial numbers. Griffin and Turpin stood nearby, talking.

"Did you find anything?" Keith asked.

"Two marijuana cigarettes and those rifles. Neither the prospect or Bonzo's old lady were here the night of the party. We've charged her with 'interfering with officers'," a disgusted Sammy Turpin explained.

"No indication of blood anywhere?" Keith asked.

"No," Turpin replied, "but the fact that the kitchen has been scrubbed is significant in itself. I've never seen such a clean kitchen in any of their hovels."

"Do we need to call in Criminalistics?" Keith asked, reaching down to massage his wounded leg.

"Yeah, but it won't do any good. The kitchen is *really* clean, right down to the pots and pans. If the body was butchered in there, we'll never know now. Maybe Fawn will come through with some information, if we sweat her a little, even though Sammy says she wasn't here the night of the fight."

"What about the prospect?"

"Naw, he wasn't here either. It was Bonzo, Wildman, and Germ—and some associate women. Say," for the first time Sammy seemed to notice the investigator's appearance, "what happened to you?"

"A close encounter with a dog. If you don't mind, I'll let the two of you question Fawn. I'm going to the hospital, then I'm going to take the evening off."

"Sure, Gary," Doyle said. "By the way, you looked just like a movie cop when you sailed out that window."

"Thanks, Doyle. I appreciate that."

Chapter Twelve

"I don't *know* what happened to Larry Foglesong's motorcycle. It broke down near the clubhouse about a month ago. Bonzo and Germ picked it up. They said they'd have it fixed, and I haven't seen Larry since then."

Fawn Delaney had been a biker woman for five years. She was still pretty at twenty-one, but one had to look close. Years of drugs and dancing in nude bars had taken the shine off.

"Tell us what you know about Larry Foglesong," Doyle said, sipping coffee from a delicate mug, which he had made.

"He's a half-wit. Spends most of his Social Security check on booze and drugs. He hangs around the clubhouse trying to score with the mamas."

"He ever score with you, Fawn?" Turpin asked.

"Hell no! I'm not a mama. I'm Bonzo's old lady!" Her face flamed as Turpin hit a nerve. "Old ladies," like Fawn, had status of sorts in the club. Mamas (also called "sheep") were available for anyone, including visitors.

"Tell me what happened that night, Fawn. What were Bonzo and Larry Foglesong fighting about?"

"Look, Sammy, I told ya . . . some brother stopped off that night. I wasn't there, so I don't even know who he was. They might notta told me, even if I hadda been there. Bonzo fights with everybody—you know that. He's been busted to prospect twice, 'cause he's so hot-tempered."

"I think it got out of hand that night, Fawn. I think maybe Bonzo went too far," Turpin continued.

"Look, I don't know whatcha gettin' at, but I'm through talkin'. You got me on a piddlin' disorderly conduct charge. Set my bond, so I can get out."

"Fawn, what if we book you for bein' an accessory to first degree murder? That wouldn't be piddlin' at all, would it?" Doyle Griffin asked quietly.

Her face went pale. Public order crimes were one thing. Accessory to murder meant hard time. Her defiance vanished. "Could . . . could I have a cigarette, Detective?"

Doyle shook out one of his cigarettes and lit it for her. He waited as she took a deep drag and leaned back in her seat. "I don't know nothin' about a murder, but I'll help you if I can."

"Why did you scrub the kitchen this week?" Doyle asked. "Next to the rest of the house that kitchen shines like a new penny."

"Bonzo made me do it. He said that Tinman, our prez, would be back from Canada this week. Tinman's picky about a clean kitchen."

"Is Tinman back?" Doyle asked.

"Naw," she shook her head quietly.

"What did the kitchen look like before you scrubbed it?" Turpin asked.

"They fixed ribs the night of the party. There was barbecue sauce and meat scraps all over the place. What's this all about, Sammy? Come on!"

"Well, Fawn, we think the Devil's Sons sold Larry Foglesong's motorcycle. We think he came after it. We believe he had a fight with Bonzo and was killed. Afterwards, we think Bonzo, Germ, and Wildman cut up Larry, put the parts in silver garbage bags and scattered him all around the county."

Her head snapped up and her eyes opened wide. "You think Larry is the Jigsaw Man?"

"That's exactly what we think," Griffin answered, stubbing out his cigarette and reaching for another.

"Naw . . . it can't be. Someone woulda let it slip . . ."

"Have you seen Germ or Wildman since you got back to the clubhouse?" Turpin asked her.

"Naw, Bonzo told me they'd gone to Cincinnati."

"They go up there often?" Sammy asked.

"Yeah, they take . . . that is, Germ has people there."

"Is that where they unload the stolen Harleys?"

"Look, Sammy. I'll help if there's been a murder. But don't expect me to snitch out my family on business, all right? I got nowhere else to go."

"Fawn, we're gonna cut you loose," Griffin said. "When you find out where Bonzo is, we wanna know. If Germ or Wildman shows up, we wanna know that. If you hear anything about Larry Foglesong, call. If you screw with us, we'll put the word out that you've been our snitch all along. All they have to do is check and find out that you didn't have to make bond today. You got that?"

"We both know what happens to old ladies who roll over on bikers, don't we, Fawn?" Sammy Turpin asked.

She shook her head tiredly but did not look at them.

"I think you need to have the rabies shots," Linda Keith said, looking closely at the inflamed stitches in Gary's calf.

"I had a tetanus shot. There hasn't been a case of rabies among domestic animals in this county for ten years."

"Well," she stood up and placed her hands on her hips. He hated it when she did that. A tall, regal woman, she had done a little modeling, but with both parents successful doctors, she had done very little in her life that she did not want to do. "At least let me call Daddy for a second opinion."

"He'd say have the shots. Doctors have to say things like that. Then he'd talk to me about a 'respectable' profession."

"You might listen for a change. You're working well below your potential."

"Who the hell do you think is going to catch the highly intelligent criminals, if not highly intelligent cops? Crooks would run the world if we didn't get in their way!"

"Then become a lawyer and *prosecute* them. Look at you.

You could have been killed today. Daddy and Mother have offered to pay your way through law school."

"I don't want to be a lawyer. If I did, I'd pay my own way. Let's not get into *that* again."

"No, let's not. I shouldn't mention the fact that grown men ought to be over cops and robbers. You talk your own language. You laugh at horrible things that disgust other people. You handle garbage! We don't have a social life because your friends can't converse on anything but criminals and crime. You work with cultural illiterates!"

"And you work with a bunch of limp-wristed faggots who have never had a glimpse of the real world!"

"Don't call my friends faggots! What are you doing? You're supposed to stay off that leg!"

"I'm going out. You knew I was a cop when you met me. Why didn't you marry a dress designer?"

"Get back in that bed!"

"The hell with the bed. I need a drink. I need *several* drinks." He jerked on his blue jeans and a flannel shirt.

"What kind of lounge is going to let you in dressed in blue jeans?"

"Cops don't drink in lounges. They drink in *bars*."

"If you leave, I may not be here when you get back." She had her hands on her hips again.

"Into every life a little rain must fall," he retorted, limping to the door.

He held the Polaroid picture in his hand, looking at it with satisfaction for a moment, then slipped it into the white envelope. The envelope was addressed to Gary Keith, in care of the Horton County Sheriff's Department.

Cops—the high and the mighty. Let them think about *this* for a while. Let them puzzle and guess. That was all they would ever do.

He had committed the perfect crime.

Chapter Thirteen

The door opened slowly to reveal a large, blonde woman of perhaps thirty years, with her hair in braids around her head. Almost as tall as Doyle, she was well proportioned—statuesque, writers once might have called her—more like a Rubens model than a modern cover girl. Her tight silk blouse was stretched across a bosom not hindered by a bra.

"May I help you?" she asked.

"I'm Sergeant Doyle Griffin of the Horton County Sheriff's Department." He flipped open his badge case. "Are you Sarah Trinkle?"

"Yes, I am." There was no alarm or anxiety in her jade green eyes, only a mild curiosity and what appeared to be amusement.

"May I come in?"

"I have a client coming this morning," she replied, "but not immediately. Come on in."

Doyle's nostrils were assaulted by the pungent odor of herbs, some familiar, some not. It was a pleasant sensation. He quickly noted the icon of the twin god Janus hanging on the wall and the statue of Pan on the table.

"Have a seat, Sergeant, and tell me how I can help you. May I get you a cup of tea? The water is ready."

"Sure. If it's not too much trouble."

"No trouble at all." His eyes followed her as she walked across the room into the kitchenette. She was indeed a big

woman. Griffin, whose taste tended toward petite women, realized with a shock that he was becoming physically aroused.
He quickly fished around in his pocket for a notebook.

In five minutes she was on the couch across from Doyle's
chair, legs folded under her, a saucer and cup perched on her
lap. Doyle took a cautious sip.

"Good. What is it?"

"Just your basic orange pekoe with a few extras stirred in,
Sergeant. Nothing exotic."

There was silence for a moment. Doyle glanced at her face
and knew immediately that she knew what had been on his
mind as he watched her. The experienced homicide investigator and cynical student of human nature almost blushed.

"I understand that you have a friend named John Waters,
Ms. Trinkle. Is that right?"

"Call me Sarah. It's so much warmer, don't you think, Sergeant?"

"All right, Sarah. Do you know him?" He looked quickly
down at his note pad, realizing that he was not in control of
this interview.

"Yes, I do. I met him at Collier State Community College
two years ago. He was studying agriculture, and I was taking a
course in mythology. John is your classic country bumpkin,
but he's adorable. His father abused him terribly while he was
growing up. He's badly scarred, but I'm working with him."

"How's that?"

"Didn't his mother tell you I'm a witch?" She smiled
sweetly at his discomfort.

"Well . . ."

"Come now, Sergeant. May I call you Doyle?" She went on
without waiting for an answer. "You're a direct man, an honest
man, I perceive. Let's not beat around the bush. I only met
Mrs. Waters once, but I know she doesn't approve of my religion or my morals. So let's get down to what you really want
to know."

"When have you seen John? He hasn't been home in a
couple of days."

"He was here until about five this morning. I don't know where he is now. The poor boy was really upset over the officer—I guess it was you—going into his workshop without permission. He thinks he may be in trouble."

"What do you think, Sarah?" Doyle sipped at the rapidly cooling tea, beginning to feel a little more in control.

"I'm not worried. I raised a cone of power and worked a spell to protect him."

"Sarah," he smiled, "sometimes it takes more than *wantin'* something to make it true. I need to question John about the meat-cuttin' tools I found in his shop."

"Don't humor me," she said. "I've already done *more* than just want to protect him. Do you pray, Doyle?"

"Well . . . yeah, but not as often as I should."

"Do you expect God to answer your prayers?"

"That's up to God, I suppose. Let's get on—"

"Well, I *don't* pray. However, I do worship. Then I take principles handed down from time immemorial and *make* things happen. I don't wait for a deity to answer my petition. I exercise the *power.* John Waters is safe from all harm right now."

"What kind of power, Sarah?" He was sidetracked, he knew, but fascinated.

"Doyle, there is no such thing as good power or bad power, only your basic power. Wise men and women have practiced a craft called *Wicca* since the beginning of time. It is the Old Religion. It predates Christianity and all the other so-called major religions." Her green eyes were drilling into his.

"I've read a little," he said, "about witches, warlocks, and devil worship—"

"You've read *very* little, I see." She laughed softly and melodiously. "Male witches are called witches. The term *warlock* was created by the church, along with the devil. They gave the devil the attributes of Pan," she pointed towards the statue. "Horns and hooves."

"This is very interesting, Sarah," he turned uncomfortably in his seat, aware that he was sweating profusely. For a brief moment, he had an irrational terror that the tea was affecting him, "but I need to talk about John."

"All right, Doyle, but would you mind if I heated up something to eat? I skipped breakfast, and I won't have time for a real lunch."

"Go right ahead." He followed her once again with his eyes as she went to the refrigerator. "What do you know about John's little workshop?"

"I've never been in it, but I know he keeps meat-cutting tools in there, which isn't surprising." She took a dish from the refrigerator and placed it into a microwave oven. Doyle was struck by the incongruity of a microwave oven among the herbs and ancient symbols.

"How's that?"

"When John went into the navy, they taught him meatcutting. It was the first time in his life that he ever did anything on his own. It was a sort of victory over his father. Naturally he clings to his first triumph. He still does special cuts of meats for his friends sometimes."

"Are you a psychologist, too?"

"As a matter of fact, I'm a state certified therapist, with a master's in psychology. Want to see my diplomas?" The bell on the microwave jingled. She removed the steaming dish, put it on a platter, and carried it into the living room.

"No, I'll take your word. What did John talk about while he was here?"

"Mostly about the fact that his privacy was invaded. He's also worried about his tools. He takes great pride in them. In fact, you've probably found by now that they are *absolutely* clean—without a trace of blood on them. John is meticulous about his tools."

"Did John give you any idea where he might be spending his time?" Griffin hoped his eyes had not given him away. It was a fact that the tools had been totally clean.

"No."

"Would you tell me, if you knew?"

"No." She forked out a tiny bit of meat and put it delicately between her teeth.

"That smells delicious," Doyle said. "What is it?"

"Leftover meat pie—liver, heart, and sweetbread. Would you like to try some?" She smiled at him brightly, her jade green eyes seeming to pull him towards her, frustrating his best efforts to conduct a no-nonsense interview.

"Maybe in a minute," he said. "Now, tell me more about these 'special cuts' that John does for his friends."

"Of course," she replied, taking another delicate bite and looking at him through lowered lids.

"You took your sweet time," Bonzo said, climbing into the pickup truck.

"I was afraid the cops were still watchin' me," Fawn answered, shifting into low gear with a grinding sound.

"Remind me to have someone stash a kerosene heater in that basement. It got cold last night."

"Well, it saved you anyway. Was there plenty to eat?"

"Yeah. I have to admit it was a good idea. If I hadn't been able to hide, the cops would have had me for sure."

Fawn had conceived the idea of a "safe house" in an abandoned building six blocks away from the clubhouse. It was the first time anyone had used it.

"What did they charge you with?"

"Disorderly conduct."

"Where'd you get the bail money?" he asked suspiciously.

"I had some saved from the household money," she lied. Wrath would fall on her, but it was better than admitting that they had turned her loose without bail.

"What do they want with me?" He let the subject of money go for the moment.

"They're looking for Larry Foglesong's motorcycle. They think you got it."

"Damn! I've got to make a couple of calls. Let's go to the Dixie Motel. I want a hot shower too."

105

"That ain't the worst of it, Bonzo."

"So what else?"

"The cops think you killed Larry Foglesong because he found out you'd ripped off his bike."

"The bastards are lookin' for me on a *murder* charge?"

"Yeah. It was Larry's body that turned up in the garbage bags."

"Sonofabitch! I've got to get out of town until this blows over. No! I got to get to Scooters Unlimited first. Nate may still have that motorcycle around the shop."

"So you *did* rip off Larry's bike?"

"Yeah, what about it?" He turned on her, eyes flashing.

"Did you . . ." she swallowed hard. "Did you kill him and cut him up too?"

"Stop this truck, bitch!" he screamed.

She pulled jerkily to the side of the road. He ripped open her blouse and ran his hands around her torso, then tore open the front of her jeans.

"Whatcha doin'?" she cried, pulling the blouse back over her bare breasts as an old man in a beat-up Chevy drove by, looking at her with interest.

"Lookin' for a wire, you dumb bitch. You know better than to ask me questions about business. Who the hell do you think you are?"

"I'm your old lady," she said, beginning to sob. "That usta mean somethin' to you. How can you say I'm wearin' a wire for cops?"

"Sorry, babe. Let's get to the motel. I gotta get hold of Nate before the cops find that scooter of Foglesong's."

She put the truck in gear and pulled away from the shoulder. It was obvious that he was not really sorry. Besides, he had not answered her question at all.

Bonzo was in deeper than theft charges this time. She had no intention of taking a long fall for a man who did not even trust her.

Chapter Fourteen

"Well, did you turn anything today?" Doyle asked, lighting a cigarette as his partner came into the office, limping slightly from the dog bite.

"No. I canvassed every house within a quarter of a mile of the quarry. Nobody admits to having seen any kind of vehicle going in or out that night. How did your interview with the witch go?"

"Not bad. I have a strong suspicion about this John Waters, though. I didn't tell his girlfriend what I wanted, and she didn't volunteer any information."

"So, what's a real witch like?" Keith asked, taking a diet soda from the small refrigerator.

"This one made my old flagpole stand up and salute," Griffin said. "She ain't even my type—big, blonde, busty—but sexy."

"Maybe she hexed you?"

"Naw, but she did feed me."

"What does a witch feed a cop?"

"A meat and spice pie," Doyle said, "and it was delicious."

"Did she tell you where to find Waters?"

"No, but I get the idea he's a mama's boy. He'll probably go home and his mother'll call us. If not, we'll wait a couple of days and stake out Sarah's house. That's the witch's name, Sarah. I think old John Waters may have done the deed."

"Maybe," Keith shrugged, "but I'm going to withhold judgment until I find Bonzo. I think he's still the best suspect. Oh, by the way—got in some reports."

"Fill me in," Griffin said. "I'm not up to reading right now."

"First of all, Criminalistics reported on Foglesong's car. It checked clean. Also, they said the rounds in the torso matched the target pistol. We can officially eliminate the rounds as cause of death. Then the lab called and said to tell you that they couldn't get a trace of anything on the butcher knives. Clean as a whistle. Funny thing, though. Those cutting tools found under the bridge had blood on them. It's the same type as Foglesong's. Couldn't raise any prints."

"Interesting," Griffin replied, "but until we have a definite suspect, there's not much to do but hang on to 'em, I guess."

The phone jangled and Keith picked it up. "Homicide, Keith."

"All right," Keith said reluctantly. "Send her on back."

"You look like somebody just licked the stripe off your candy, Gary. What's wrong?"

"Larry Foglesong's mother is here. I haven't been looking forward to this."

"She the hysterical type?"

"Hasn't been so far . . . at least not over the phone, but I dread it anyway."

"It goes with the territory," Griffin said as the woman rapped lightly at the door.

Deloris Foglesong was a tall, sophisticated woman in her mid-fifties. She was dressed expensively and her hair was in place, looking as if she had just left the beauty parlor. She shook hands firmly as Keith introduced her to Griffin.

"Please have a seat, Mrs. Foglesong," Gary said.

"Thank you, Officer Keith. I won't take up much of your time. I just want to know exactly what was done to my boy, and what you've discovered so far."

"Well . . . Larry was . . ." Keith was not exactly sure how to go about describing the butchery to the mother of the victim.

"Someone apparently murdered your son, Mrs. Foglesong, by drivin' a sharp object into his eye socket, penetratin' the brain. Afterwards, they cut his body into fragments, put them in silver garbage bags, and distributed them around the county."

Gary Keith stood in shock at Griffin's almost off-hand description of what had happened. The woman merely nodded, however.

"The papers said something about gunshots, I believe."

"We've eliminated the gunshots as a cause of death," Griffin said. He explained what had happened.

"What about my son's belongings?"

"Apparently he took them with him when he left. His car was at his last residence," Keith answered.

"Will you see that his roommates keep that old car? I have no use for it. You've both been very kind." She stood and shook hands again. "I'll arrange to have my son's body sent home after the coroner releases it. I trust you'll call when you've tracked down my son's killer?"

"We'll do that," Doyle promised quietly.

They sat in silence for a few minutes after she left. Then Keith spoke. "A real gutsy lady."

"Yeah, she is," Doyle replied.

"Mail call." They looked up as their chubby, cheerful secretary entered. She handed Gary a long envelope, made a kissing sound, then left.

Keith ripped off the end and shook out the contents. They both sat staring at it. Larry Foglesong's head stared at them from the glossy surface of a Polaroid picture. The photograph had been taken from much too close. Everything was blurred, except for his face. It was, however, unmistakably the severed head of the victim.

"I'll be damned!" Doyle exhaled slowly. "Somene is pulling our tails."

"Yes," Keith agreed.

"Do you kinda get a feelin' that you ought to recognize that picture? Like maybe you've seen it before?" Griffin asked.

"No, I can't say that I do."

"I don't know what it is, but I feel like I've seen it before
. . . like I should *remember* something about it."

"Well," Keith picked it up by the edge, "I'm going to take it
back to Criminalistics and see what they can find. If we're
lucky, he left us a print."

Doyle sat quietly, smoking and sipping coffee after his partner left. There was definitely something about that picture.

Oh, well, he thought. *It will come to me eventually. It always does.*

　　　　　John Waters sat quietly on the ridge overlooking
his mother's house. He had been there all day. There were no
cops watching; he was certain of that. He would have spotted
them by now.

His mother was gone to church. She went *every* Wednesday.
There would be nobody to see him slip into his shop. He was
expecting a visitor. It was his regular night. It would be necessary to call things off for a while, but he would finish up this
one.

He went back to the large butcher knife that he had been
sharpening, his big hands rhythmically pulling the blade back
and forth across the whetstone. The knife was not nearly as
good as the ones the cops had seized, but it would do the job.
There was also a small hacksaw in his bag.

John had been really frightened at first, but Sarah had convinced him that everything would be all right. After all, he
had always cleaned up, leaving no traces whatsoever in his
workshop.

Besides, Sarah had the power to protect him. She had
promised. He would slip back after he had finished tonight
and would sleep beside her warm body.

He would also take her a present, and tomorrow she could
fix another of her special meat pies: liver, heart, and sweetbread, which he would eat to please her.

Chapter Fifteen

Gary Keith opened his front door and reached in to turn on the light. He hoped Linda had calmed down. She had been asleep when he returned from Neptune's Lounge the night before, and she had not stirred as he slipped out early that morning. His career was the source of a long-time argument, but things had always worked out before.

The overhead light came on, but not the two lamps. When his eyes adjusted, he saw why. The only two things left in the living room were the telephone and his bookcase. The rest of the furniture was gone, leaving little indentations in the carpet where the legs had sunk in. Even the pictures were gone from the walls.

Walking through the rest of the house, he found it empty also, except for the occasional item that he had brought to the marriage: books, an antique rifle on the wall, his collection of ceramic pigs. In the bedroom, he found his old sleeping bag neatly laid out where the bed had been.

Above the sleeping bag, taped to the wall, was a note neatly written in Linda's special violet ink: "Dear Gary: Enough is enough. Call one of your cop buddies if you get lonesome. Sincerely, Linda."

Leaving the note on the wall, he went into the kitchen, opened the cabinet over the refrigerator, and took down an unopened bottle of cognac. He had been saving it for a special occasion. This seemed as good a time as any.

111

Opening another cabinet, he found that the crystal was gone. She had, however, left the plastic tumblers. He twisted the top off the cognac, poured a large slug, and swallowed. The fumes filled his sinus cavities, bringing tears to his eyes and burning all the way down. He poured another swig and repeated the process.

Somehow he had expected more class from Linda than this. He knew such things happened every day, but to other people. He had seen it a thousand times as a cop. Still, he had expected better from a woman with her cultural background.

He slid down the wall and stretched his legs out in front of him. Pouring himself another drink, he set the bottle between his legs and began to weep quietly. He had to get it out of his system; otherwise he might break down later in front of her when the divorce papers were being signed.

When she saw him again, the mask would definitely be in place; the cold, hard cop stare would tell her that her absence meant nothing to him.

It was the only manly way to handle it.

"Tell me about it," Lieutenant Howard Mull asked, popping the cap off a bottle of imported German beer. "How close are you?"

"I don't know, Howard. We've got two good suspects, but there's still a way to go," Doyle Griffin replied. He had come home to find his supervisor waiting outside, a bag of imported beer under his arm. Doyle had never liked imported beer, but he drank it rather than offend Mull.

"Well, I'm listening," Mull said, taking a sip, then smacking his lips.

"Gary thinks Foglesong was killed by a biker called Bonzo to cover up a motorcycle theft. Sammy Turpin saw a fight at the Devil's Sons' clubhouse a day or two before the body was found. It's possible, but I'm not real excited about it. Not yet, anyway. If we turn up the motorcycle, maybe."

"What do you think, Doyle?"

"I've got an eccentric meatcutter with a girlfriend who's a

genuine, practicing witch. He disposed of bloody clothes around the time of the murder, and his mother found silver garbage bags under the sink. The bags are the same brand, but they sell 'em in every grocery store in the country. I couldn't get anything from his tools, but he's been missin' since the day I went up there."

"Doesn't sound like a lot of progress."

"I guess not. On top of everything else, the killer has sent us a Polaroid picture of the victim's head. He's pullin' our tails."

"What could you tell from the picture?"

"Nothin' really. It was shot so close that everything is out of focus, except the face itself. I got a feelin', though, about that picture—"

"What about it?"

"I don't know, Howard." Griffin turned up the bottle and finished the beer. "There's somethin' gnawin' at me. The picture tells me more than I *see*. Know what I mean?"

"Yes, there's a detail that your unconscious mind is picking up on, but your conscious hasn't caught on yet. It happened to me once. I smelled an odor at the scene of a rape-murder that I couldn't put my finger on. Almost a month later, my wife was baking a cake. I watched her for a minute, then it came to me—vanilla extract. That was what I had smelled. The killer worked in a bakery. He caved in as soon as I confronted him with it."

"I guess you're right, Howard. It'll come to me."

"Sure it will. Just relax and don't try so hard." He raised his hand as his cheek twitched for the first time that evening. He shook his head ruefully. "I guess I'm not the one to give advice on relaxation."

A light knocking sound came from the back door, and Griffin got up to open it. A dark-haired woman of about twenty-five stepped in, stood on tip-toes, and kissed Griffin. Then, seeing Mull for the first time, she blushed.

"Trish," Griffin said, "this is my lieutenant, Howard Mull. Howard, this is Trish Walker."

"I recognize her from the evening news. You're even prettier in person, Miss Walker." He stood up.

"Call me Trish, and don't leave on my account. I just dropped by for a few minutes."

"And you call me Howard. But I was ready to go anyway. An old man like me needs his rest. It was nice to have met you."

Griffin walked Mull to the front door and opened it for him. "You sly dog," the lieutenant said. "All this time I thought you lived like a monk. How did you ever manage a woman with that much class?"

"They don't call me the 'Silver-tongued Devil' for nothin'," the detective chuckled. "Though if I don't get this case solved and spend some time with her, she's gonna look somewhere else."

"Son, my suggestion is that you learn priorities, or you'll end up old and with a twitch in your face. And I can tell you this: that girl standing in your kitchen is a definite priority."

"All right, Lieutenant. How about a coupla days off?"

"Sorry, Sergeant. I'd like to do it, but you have a murder to solve," Howard Mull laughed as he spoke over his shoulder.

Midget Poplin and Jumbo Patterson were parked behind an abandoned service station, their cars pulled up next to each other, facing in opposite directions. They were doing what patrol officers generally do on slow nights when there is no supervisor around. They were goofing off, drinking coffee.

"As far as I'm concerned, Midget, the only round suitable for police work is the .45 caliber."

"Why do you say that? The .38 has been the basic police round since police departments were first formed in this country."

"Because when you shoot a guy with a .45 he goes down every time—even if you just hit him in the hand or somethin'."

"Jumbo, that's a lot of crap. I don't know why intelligent people keep on saying things like that. The whole idea violates the laws of physics," Midget said.

"Whatta you mean, it violates the laws of physics? What's physics got to do with bullets?"

"You ever had physics in school, Jumbo?"

"Naw, I didn't like science." He took a sip of his coffee, wondering where the conversation was going.

"Well, you should have. You'd have learned that for every action there is an equal reaction."

"So what does that mean?"

"All right," Midget was waving his hands as he always did when involved in making a point, "if the bullet from a .45 moves forward fast enough to knock a 200-pound man backwards twenty feet, the *reaction* should knock the man who fires the pistol back the *exact same distance*. It's a law of physics."

"Naw," Jumbo said, wadding up his styrofoam cup and throwing it out the window, "the guy doing the shooting is braced and ready for it."

"It doesn't make any difference if he braced or not. The reaction is the same. Look—"

"Alpha 11," the radio crackled, interrupting Midget's lecture.

"Alpha 11," Jumbo replied, "go ahead."

"Signal 6, or advise a number," the dispatcher told him.

"Now, what the hell has she got that's so important she can't say it over the radio?" Jumbo grumbled, starting his cruiser.

"Maybe your girlfriend's got the clap?" Midget smirked, tossing out his coffee and preparing to follow his big friend off the lot.

"Only if she'd been seeing you on the side," Jumbo yelled out the window.

They pulled into the lot of a closed market about a mile away. A young man with long, stringy hair and a beard was in the phone booth. Both officers got out and stood by the door, however, staring at him without speaking. In less than a minute he nervously ended his call. Slipping by them, he walked up the road muttering profanities under his breath, which they

115

chose to ignore. Jumbo radioed in the number of the phone booth. A moment later it rang.

"Alpha 11," he said, "What've you got that's so important that I had to interrupt a sexual interlude?" He listened quietly for a moment, his brows coming together in concentration. "No kidding. I'm on my way. Alpha 9 will be going with me."

"What is it?" Poplin asked.

"Some kids on Bell's Valley Road think they've found another torso."

Alpha 3, Sergeant Vince Jordan, hated it when the dispatchers gave out "secret" calls by telephone. It was perfectly within departmental guidelines, but he hated it anyway. He believed a supervisor should always have the option of changing the dispatcher's orders. The dispatchers all referred to Jordan as "Sergeant Butt-insky," or the "mobile dispatcher."

Generally, the reason for dispatching by phone was to avoid having the news media descend on the crime scene. Sometimes, however, it was for personal reasons: the officer had a problem at home or a date with the dispatcher.

"Alpha 11," Sergeant Jordan said, "go to channel 2 Kilo."

"Alpha 11, to Alpha 3," Jumbo Patterson said shortly.

"Have you been given a call, Alpha 11?"

"10–4, Sergeant."

"Can you advise the nature of the call?"

"Negative, Sergeant. The dispatcher advised me not to broadcast it." Jumbo knew that to alert reporters listening to scanners, the sergeant might as well have rung a signal bell. They would all be locked in now, listening breathlessly.

"Give me the location, Alpha 11," Jordan demanded.

"Sergeant . . . uh, the dispatcher advised us to check before calling additional units to the scene."

"Alpha 11, I *am* the supervisor in charge at this time. You *will* give me the location."

"10–4," Jumbo said reluctantly, knowing what he was about to unleash. "We're en route to Bell's Valley, about a mile off Halston Pike."

Jumbo had barely finished speaking before three camera crews and reporters from both newspapers were rolling toward the scene.

Sergeant Jordan, perfectly aware what he had done, smiled a tight little smile. He was of the opinion that homicide investigators stole entirely too much of the media glory. Tonight it would be different.

"By God, it *does* look like a torso," Midget Poplin said, peering through his binoculars across a marshy wooded area to a small creek. "It looks like a female torso."

"I tol'ja, dind't I?" the ten-year-old boy gloated. "It's a body, and I seen it first." The small boy with bushy hair stood with a group of eight or more children. His mother had called the sheriff's department at his insistence.

"It's gettin' dark," Jumbo said. "I guess we'd better wade out through this swamp and take a closer look."

"I guess so," Midget replied, "but I ain't lookin' forward to it."

At that moment Sergeant Jordan's cruiser slid around the curve. He jumped out, straightening his uniform.

"Well, what is it?"

"Seems to be a female torso, Sergeant, but it's gettin' dark. We're gonna wade out and take a look."

"Give me those binoculars!" He peered intently across the marshy area, then turned quickly.

"Clear all these people out of here, right now." He indicated the clump of children across the road. "Let's get this crime scene secured."

"Sergeant," Jumbo said, "hadn't we better take a closer look before it gets dark?"

"You can't just *trample* a crime scene. We'll look, after everything's secured."

"Sergeant," Midget said, "it seems to me that we're more likely to trample things in the dark than now. Besides, the media's gonna be all over us in a few mintues."

117

"Get this crowd moved away. I'll handle the media if the need arises."

The two officers began to move the children away, both sighing deeply. They had been around sergeants long enough to be convinced they couldn't be told anything. Just then, true to prediction, the media crews arrived and began setting up cameras and sound equipment before the officers could move the crowd. Sergeant Jordan was standing before the cameras, straightening his navy blue on navy blue tie.

"What do you have here, Sergeant?" one of the reporters asked.

"It would appear that we have here the second in a possible series of mutilation murders. The officers are about to go into this swampy area and take a look."

"So you don't actually *know* what it is, then?" another reporter asked.

"Well," the sergeant smiled as if addressing a small child, "through the field glasses we saw a set of what appeared to be human breasts on a body with no head, arms, or legs. What do *you* think it is?"

"Go ahead and check it, men. Don't disturb the crime scene," Jordan ordered, tugging at his gunbelt and glancing at the camera.

Midget and Jumbo started across the field, stepping in puddles of water that they could no longer see because of the dimming light.

"That idiot!" Midget hissed under his breath. "A few minutes ago, we could have *seen* these puddles."

It took them eight or ten minutes to thread their way across the marsh. For a moment they looked across the creek at the torso, then started down the bank toward the water. Suddenly the area was flooded with light. Sergeant Jordan had aimed a 300,000-candle-power light at them. Both were blinded momentarily.

"I hope there ain't no more parts floatin' around in here," Jumbo muttered, stepping into water up to his knees. Midget followed him, and they waded across.

"Don't worry," Midget suddenly snickered. "If there are any more parts, we'll glue'm back."

He reached out and thumped the "torso." It was a department store mannequin.

"Damn," Jumbo swore, reaching for his radio.

"Wait. I got an idea."

At the road, Sergeant Jordan picked up his radio. "Alpha 3 to Alpha 11, have you made contact yet?"

There was no answer as Jordan continued to focus his hand-held light on the point where the officers had walked over the embankment.

"Look!" one of the reporters suddenly shouted. "They're coming out."

"And they're carrying the torso," another yelled, "by the neck and the crotch!"

Had it not been dark, everyone could have seen the color drain from Sergeant Jordan's face. *Those two idiots have moved a body from a murder scene!* he thought. He, Sergeant Jordan, was in charge. *He* would write the memos. *He* would take the blame.

"Sergeant," a plump, blonde woman asked, "isn't it normal practice to leave a body in place for homicide and the coroner to check out?"

Jordan opened his mouth, but no words came out. He turned and watched with everyone else as the officers walked through the marshy field, making sucking sounds in the wet grass. When they were within fifteen feet of the bank, they stopped and hurled the "torso" at the crowd. The reporters and the sergeant all backed up as it skittered across the pavement with a hollow sound.

"Sergeant," Midget said with a big smile, "I do believe *rigor mortis* has set in."

Seeing what it was, the reporters began to giggle, then laugh out loud. Sergeant Jordan was quietly edging back to his car. He was almost there when the reporter who had made the comment about not actually *knowing* what was in the creek yelled at his back.

"I personally think it's a department store mannequin, Sergeant. What do *you* think it is?"

Jordan drove away quickly, the sound of their laughter echoing in his ears. For once, the homicide officers did not get all the glory.

Chapter Sixteen

"This is a bad idea, Bonzo," Fawn said as they coasted down the hill in the old pickup truck. "If we get caught, you're going to look guiltier than ever."

"Shut up, bitch. I've got to find out if Nate's still got parts of that half-wit's bike in the shop."

"Why don't we just wait until Nate gets back?" Fawn shuddered nervously.

"Because I don't even know where he is. Pretty soon the cops are gonna find out about Scooters Unlimited, and when they do, Nate'll burn us to save himself. If there are any parts of that motorcycle left, I'm gonna get 'em out. Just don't ask me any more questions!"

Bonzo steered the old truck behind the ramshackle clapboard building. The Devil's Sons and Nate Perry, owner of the repair shop, had made good money. The bikers delivered stolen Harley-Davidson motorcycles, and Nate turned them into parts, which were then sold in Cincinnati and other cities. He had not invested any money, however, in the upkeep of the rented building.

One of the problems the Devil's Sons had with Nate was his penchant for taking off without telling anyone. He was apt to go fishing without notice, but they put up with him because they were not in a position to advertise for associates.

"Wait in the truck," Bonzo said, reaching behind the seat for a crowbar and flashlight. "I won't be too long. If you see any police cars go by, tap the horn real easy and get the hell away for a while."

John Waters carried the last heavy bag from his workshop and handed it to the man standing inside the van. The man's face was hidden by the darkness. John had never seen him in the daylight.

"That's it," Waters said.

"Same time next week?"

"No. I'll leave a message on the board at the laundromat when I'm ready to work again."

"We can't have that. We need somebody dependable."

"I *am* dependable, but the cops are watching me. Do you want them to find out what I've been cuttin' up in there, and what you and your crew do with 'em?"

"Why didn't you warn me?" the man hissed. "I wouldn't have been here tonight."

"Don't worry. I've watched from the woods all day. Just make sure you dispose of the remains a long ways from here."

"You shouldn't have taken the chance tonight," the man whispered angrily.

"There was no way to contact you, now, was there?"

"I guess not."

"My old lady is the only person within a mile of here, anyway. She sleeps like a dead person. Get going, I gotta clean up this blood. I'll leave a message when it's safe to start back."

As John Waters watched the van move cautiously down the long driveway without lights, his mother was dialing the telephone. He was right about her sound sleep, but he had forgotten about her bursitis.

The pain in her shoulder had awakened her. After she retrieved her medicine from the shelf over the kitchen sink, she was drawing a glass of water when she saw the van moving across the moonlit barnyard. He was there! John was in his workshop!

Her own son or not, she had no intention of ending up like the man in the quarry.

*   *   *

"Uhmmmmm, I've missed that," Trish Walker murmured, rolling over on her back. "If you don't solve this jigsaw case pretty soon, my frustration is going to interfere with my cheerful disposition, and my ratings are going to fall." A thin sheen of sweat glistened across her bare breasts.

"*You've* missed it," Doyle exclaimed. "I was gettin' as tense as a rabbit in a dog lot."

"Well, I trust your tensions have dissolved—at least temporarily."

"Yeah, maybe I can remember what I ought to be rememberin' about that picture that came in the mail." He reached over to the bedside table, shook a cigarette out of the crumpled pack, and lit it.

"You know you're going to die if you don't get off those cigarettes, don't you?"

"I reckon I'm gonna die, even if I *do* get off them."

"Don't be flip about it. I'm serious."

"So am I. Are you hungry?" he asked, changing the subject before it could get out of hand.

She sighed deeply and shook her head. The cigarettes had been a bone of contention throughout their relationship. "Yes, I am, Officer. What did you have in mind?"

"Well, I was thinkin' about turnip greens, fried ham, and maybe white beans and cornbread."

"You don't even *like* country cooking," she said, pulling his hair.

"I know, but it's bad for the country-boy image to ask for caviar and snails."

"All right, where can we eat this time of morning?"

"Let's try that all-night cafe on Union. They serve spicy Greek food. I had some meat pie yesterday. It whetted my appetite for spicy dishes."

"That's fine with me. What are the odds that we'll be able to finish the meal?"

"It's after 2:00 A.M. now. I don't expect that anything's

gonna happen at this time of morning. Come on, let's get dressed."

As Doyle was reaching for his trousers, the phone rang.

"Damn," he swore, picking up the receiver. "This is Griffin. Go ahead and ruin my night." He listened intently.

"You didn't put any of that on the air, did you? Damn! That was stupid! The media will be all over us. I'll need all the units you can spare, includin' one just to keep the reporters out of our hair. I'm on my way."

"What is it?" Trish asked as he slammed the phone down.

"The mother of one of my suspects in the jigsaw case just called dispatch. Her son's at the house now, or in his butcher shop, anyway. The dispatcher told the patrol officer en route that he's a suspect—over the air. I don't know what they use for brains in dispatch."

He jerked on his pants and reached for the shirt.

"It sounds like an honest mistake to me," she mused. "What kind of problems can it cause?"

"Oh nothin'," Doyle retorted, "except that when patrol roars down on him like gangbusters, it may scare him so bad that he flees my jurisdiction. Or even worse, what if he gets shot, or somethin'?"

John Waters heard the crunch of tires on the long gravel driveway. He put down the squeegee and walked to the door. His knives were washed and polished and the stainless steel table was clean, but there was still blood all over the tiled floor. Who would be coming up the driveway at this time of morning?

He walked to the door and squinted down the driveway. A car bumped into sight, but before it was close enough for him to get a good look at it in the dark, a spotlight fell on him, outlining him in the doorway of the barn.

Cops! He dropped the squeegee and ran back into his workshop. Picking up the knives he had brought from Sarah's and the package he had wrapped for her, he bolted out of the barn just as the officer got out of his cruiser. The headlights of a second car topped the hill behind the first.

"Hey, you!" the patrolman yelled. "Hold it right there."

John ran, remarkably fast for such a big, hulking individual. Like a beagle on a rabbit's trail, the patrol officer followed, though at the moment he had nothing but a reasonable suspicion that something was wrong.

"Alpha 12," he yelled into his radio as he ran. "I'm in foot pursuit . . . white male, big man . . . knife in his hands . . . back-up check a room in the barn . . . light's on there."

"10–4, Alpha 12. Did you copy, Alpha 7? Check the room in the barn. All other units in the area, assist 12 and 7. They are in foot pursuit of a possible murder suspect."

"Alpha 7," the second officer said a moment later, "there's not anyone in the barn, but there's blood all over the place. The next unit needs to secure this room for homicide. I'm goin' after Alpha 12 and the suspect."

"10–4, Alpha 7."

John ran through the woods, his breath burning his lungs, but he was putting distance between himself and the cops. They were probably younger and more athletic, but he was on familiar ground.

He could hear the cops behind him, thrashing into brush and once even a barbed-wire fence. They had been close enough for him to hear one of them cursing as he ripped his flesh and trousers.

Sliding down an embankment, he slipped into the cold, fast-moving water of a creek. If they called in dogs, they would lose his trail here. He knew where he was going, and the dogs would not be able to track him there.

He had spent too many boyhood days roaming these hills to be caught by a couple of city boys and their fancy dogs. He would get away.

But what am I going to do next? he thought. *They'll be watching Sarah's house.* He knew they would also be analyzing the blood he'd left all over the tiled floor.

Soon the police would know everything.

Chapter Seventeen

Bonzo banged his shin on the frame of a Harley-Davidson and cursed quietly to himself at the sloppiness of the mechanic who turned stolen motorcycles into parts for the Devil's Sons. He was already a mass of bruises from the foot race with the cop.

Fawn was right. This was not a good idea. With the lights on, he might have been able to locate Larry Foglesong's motorcycle, or the parts, anyway. In the dark, it was impossible. He was turning to leave when he knocked over a stack of parts. They clattered loudly all around him. Luckily, the motorcycle shop was in an isolated area.

Had it not been for the noise of the falling parts, Bonzo would have heard Fawn tap the horn lightly, as he had instructed her to do if anyone drove by.

Mike Patterson, also known as Jumbo, had seen the faint taillights of the old pickup truck as it pulled away from the isolated motorcycle shop called Scooters Unlimited. He was torn between following the truck and checking the shop.

Thieves very often dropped their confederates off, then returned to pick them up along with the loot. On the other hand, the pickup truck might have already been on the second run.

Jumbo made his decision and notified the dispatcher that he

would be out of the car checking the building. He killed his lights and eased up in the parking lot.

A faint but unmistakable light reflected off the wall of the building inside.

"Alpha 11," he called, "get me a back-up started. I've got one inside."

There was a loud clanking sound from inside as Jumbo eased along the side of the building. *Noisy thief,* he thought. Just then Jumbo tripped over a section of exhaust pipe. He froze, weapon in hand, and the noise from inside stopped.

The hasp on the rear door of the building had been pried off. Knowing that he had blown the element of surprise, Jumbo kicked the door open, then stepped quickly back in case the burglar had a firearm.

"Come on out!" Jumbo yelled. "There's nowhere to go!"

There was no sound from inside. Jumbo played his light across the inside of the building, standing to the side. Not seeing anyone, he darted to the other side of the door so he could illuminate the other part of the building.

Still he saw nothing.

The big man stood puzzled. Could he have been wrong? Was the thief already gone? Was his imagination playing tricks on him? Bending over, he picked up a large gravel and tossed it inside the building. It bounced around with a hollow sound.

He could wait. Back-up would be there shortly. On the other hand, if there was no one inside, his brother officers would give him hell—unless he canceled them first.

Pride won over good judgment.

In a crouching movement, pistol pointed forward, Jumbo stepped through the door and swung to cover the inside of the building. Bonzo, who had been standing quietly, hit Jumbo on the side of the head with a piece of angle iron.

The blow would have put an ordinary man out for the count, but Jumbo was not ordinary. He stumbled a couple of steps, then whirled, shaking his head.

Bonzo was out the door before the big cop could find a target. Amazed that Jumbo was still on his feet, he made for the woods to avoid the police. Fawn would be driving around but would be back to pick him up. All he had to do was wait.

For once, however, Bonzo had overestimated his control over the woman. She *had* turned around and come back, but when she saw the parked police car, she had made her decision. He already was a murder suspect. Most definitely he was about to be arrested for burglary.

"Fawn, baby," she muttered to herself while grinding the gears of the old pickup truck, "it's time to look out for yerself." She headed back to the Dixie Motel for her belongings. It had been a long time since she had been home to see her mother.

"Alpha 11 to Alpha 9."

"Go ahead, Alpha 11," Midget Poplin replied.

"Are you close, Midget?"

"10–4, I'm coming at you westbound, about one minute away."

"Watch for a white male. All I saw was a T-shirt with something written on the front. He's armed with some kind of metal club. He hit me in the side of the head with it. The charge will be aggravated assault. Did you copy that?"

"10–4." Midget answered. "White male, armed and dangerous."

Jumbo's transmission was meant not only to alert Midget of the suspect's dangerous nature. He wanted to establish probable cause in case further violence occurred.

"Alpha 11 to dispatch."

"Go ahead, Alpha 11."

"You'd better start me an ambulance. He whacked me pretty hard. I think I have a small cut on my head." At the emergency room later it would require eighteen stitches to close it.

"Alpha 9!" Midget's voice had risen an octave. "I've got him in sight. I'll be in foot pursuit. He's running across an open field at Coker Road and Miller Pike, southbound. He's still carrying the pipe, or whatever it is." Midget's voice had become jerky on the last few words. It was obvious he was running hard.

"Bitch! Low-life whore," Bonzo hissed to himself as he thudded across the field. She had left him! Had driven away and given him up to the cops. And after he had treated her so well. He hardly ever beat her, never loaned her out to any of the brothers, and always gave her a small share of the thousand or so a week she brought in from nude dancing.

His arms were stinging from the briars he had run through while trying to make his way back to the road. Instead of finding Fawn waiting, though, he had walked into the headlights of a cruiser. The cop driving it was closing in on Bonzo.

Bonzo had absolutely no doubt what was in store if the cop caught him. He had attacked a police officer, had maybe badly injured him. Cops understand the law of the pack. When someone hurts one of yours, you hurt him worse. It is one thing cops and bikers have in common.

The cop chasing him showed no sign of giving up. Aside from the beating he would receive, Bonzo knew they wanted him on suspicion of murder.

As he hit a stretch of waist-high grass, a desperate plan was born. Bonzo suddenly dropped and turned in the direction from which the cop was running.

He heard the footsteps come to a halt.

"Give it up!" Midget yelled. "You got nowhere to go! There are cruisers everywhere. Give up! I don't want to kill you, but I will."

Bonzo fought to control his breathing. The cop was out of breath, too. His breathing was drowning out the biker's own loud wheezes.

"I mean it," Poplin said, turning on his flashlight. "You don't want to get into a gunfight with nothing but a club." The officer advanced a few feet, playing the light throughout the tall grass.

Bonzo waited. *Just a few feet more.* He had the element of surprise.

"Stand up or I'm going to put a few rounds down in front of me. That was my friend you hit back there." The threat was an idle one. Poplin was too good an officer to fire without a clear target. He edged forward a few more feet, watching for movement.

The big biker stood up, less than ten feet from Poplin and to his right. He charged, the angle iron drawn back over his shoulder, teeth bared.

"Ahhhhrrrrrr . . ." Bonzo roared like a bull as he ran at the officer.

It seemed a slow motion scenario to Midget Poplin. His body moved as it had been trained. There was no change of stance. Swinging the pistol to the right, he fired the .38 special three times . . . from the hip.

It was nothing like the movies. The biker stopped, looking more puzzled than hurt, and the angle iron fell from his grasp. Looking down, he saw the three separate stains. He did not know that his heart already had stopped. In actuality, it no longer existed as such. Parts of it were on the ground behind him, blown out by the "plus p" rounds traveling at more than 1,200 feet per second.

He looked at Midget as if to speak, but no sound came out, only the coppery taste of blood foaming in the back of his throat. With a gurgling sound, he slowly fell forward. The officer would remember that sound as long as he lived.

"Alpha 9," Midget spoke into his radio. "Start an ambulance, a supervisor, and a homicide officer. Advise Units 1 and 2 that I have been involved in a fatal shooting."

"Unit 320 to dispatch," Doyle Griffin spoke tiredly, "call Unit 323 and wake him up. Get him en route to the shooting scene. I'll be tied up for a while."

When Doyle pulled into the driveway of the Waters' farm, Mrs. Waters was standing by the barn talking to a patrol officer. Her gray hair was pulled back in braids, and she was clutching her housecoat around her.

"He was here, Sergeant!" she said. "He was in the barn."

"Are you sure, Mrs. Waters? It could have been a prowler."

"Sergeant, Mrs. Waters has filled me in," the tall, slender patrol officer said. "Her *son* was here. Take a look in the barn."

Doyle paused at the door. The stainless steel cutting table was already spotless, but there was blood all over the floor. He had been interrupted during his cleaning.

"Alpha 12," the radio crackled. "We've lost the suspect. Get us a K-9 unit started this way."

"What did he just say?" Mrs. Waters asked from behind Doyle.

"They've lost your son. The officer just called for a dog to help track him down."

"It won't do any good," the woman was visibly shaken. "John knows these hills like the inside of his mouth. Even his daddy couldn't find him when he was of a mind to hide. I'm gonna get my stuff together and go visit my sister in Dayton until you find him. He knows by now that I turned him in."

"You're probably right, Mrs. Waters," Doyle replied.

"It's that blonde witch," she snapped. "That boy was raised in a God-fearin' home." When Doyle did not reply, she turned and went in.

"How about givin' me a hand?" Doyle said to the patrolman. "I've got pictures to take and samples to gather."

"Sure, Sarge. Is this guy the jigsaw killer?"

"Maybe," Doyle replied, "but don't say nothin' like that to the press. It's gonna be bad enough without addin' fuel to the fire."

"Unit 323, I'm on the scene," Gary Keith said.

In the field beside the road, several things were happening at once, normal procedure at the scene of a shooting. An officer was holding the camera crews and reporters back. A paramedic was kneeling over the downed outlaw biker, shaking his head. Another paramedic was trying to get Jumbo into the ambulance to patch his head, but the big officer was ignoring the paramedic. He had his arm around Midget and was explaining that there was no way he could have done anything but shoot. Midget—his face white—did not appear convinced.

"Looks like this one could have gone either way," Gary Keith commented looking at the piece of angle iron by Bonzo's body.

"Yeah," Jumbo said, "there's still blood and hair on that piece of steel where he hit me back at Scooters Unlimited."

"Where?" Keith asked.

"Scooters Unlimited."

"Is that one of the places where the Devil's Sons hang out?"

"Yeah, I've seen the scrounges around there before," Jumbo replied.

"Is anyone watching it now?"

"No. Dispatch is tryin' to locate the owner."

Keith spoke into his radio. "323 to dispatch."

"Go ahead, 323."

"Get a cruiser back to Scooters Unlimited. I want it secured. Nobody—not even the owner—is to enter until I check it out."

"10–4, 323."

"What is it?" Jumbo asked.

"There may be part of Larry Foglesong's bike in there. The Devil's Sons may have sent somebody to clean up the evidence."

"Naw, they didn't *send* anybody."

"What do you mean?" the investigator asked.

"That's Bonzo on the ground there. I thought you'd seen him before."

Gary Keith walked over and looked carefully at the dead biker's face, then shook his head, turning around to face the other two officers. It was, indeed, the man he had chased for several blocks less than two days earlier.

"You know," he said quietly, "they look a lot different alive."

132

Chapter Eighteen

Doyle Griffin sipped his fifteenth cup of coffee and lit his forty-second cigarette since having been called by dispatch the previous night. He watched Gary Keith filling out a mound of reports. Beside Keith's desk was a Harley-David-son frame, crowded between two cabinets.

"So that's it, huh?" Doyle asked. "The frame to Foglesong's motorcycle?"

"Yes. I'll draw up warrants in a little while, charging the owner of Scooters Unlimited with receiving and concealing stolen property. I think he'll be more than glad to connect Bonzo to Foglesong's bike—for consideration, of course. I think this one's about wrapped up."

"Never count your chickens before you smell 'em fryin'," Doyle countered, propping his feet up on the desk. "I hope you're right, but I'm still bankin' on John Waters bein' involved."

"What happened up there last night? I was so busy, I didn't pay much attention."

"The K-9 man says he took to the creek. There are all sorts of places he coulda climbed out by usin' tree limbs. No way the dog could find him. He left blood all over the floor this time, though. I at least got some samples. I should know somethin' by the end of the week."

"Do you think Waters is connected to the bikers, maybe through his girlfriend? Sammy Turpin says a lot of bikers are into the occult."

"Who knows?" Doyle answered, stubbing out one cigarette and lighting another. "One thing I do know. The bikers will be scarcer than hair on a frog's chest for the next little while. They'll crawl into the cracks."

"Yeah. Guess so, Doyle. So where do we go from here?"

"Well, youngster, I'm goin' home and get some sleep and snugglin' with my sweetie for a few hours. You've done a good job. I'd suggest you take a break tonight, too. Tomorrow I'll take another run up to the witch's house to see if I can locate John Waters. He'll turn up there eventually."

Keith agreed. "By the way, the garage called. They want to know what to do with Larry Foglesong's car."

"I forgot about that," Doyle answered. "Mrs. Foglesong said to give it to Larry's roommates. Tell the garage to deliver it there. I don't know what they'll do about a title. I guess it won't matter much."

"Well," Griffin stood up, "I'm headin' out for some sleep, a few beers, and some cuddlin'. All work and no play makes Jack a dull boy. That goes for you, too."

If Griffin had looked back, he would have been surprised to see tears in Gary Keith's eyes. The investigator had not even told his partner that he now lived in a house with almost no furniture and no wife.

"Well, I'm proud of my little buddy. He'll be proud of hisself when the shock of blowin' Bonzo's heart out passes." Jumbo took a big swig of beer and wiped his mouth with the back of his hand. A shaved spot on the side of his head showed black stitches stark against the white skin.

"Looks like you had a pretty close call," David Lark commented, looking at the stitches.

"Naw," Jumbo replied, "he woulda had to hit somethin' more delicate than my head to do me any damage. It bent that angle iron, you know."

All of them laughed uproariously, though it would not have seemed so funny without the preceding three beers. It was the usual crowd, minus Midget: Jumbo, David Lark, and Hank Pike.

"Well, I say, here's to the Midget for riddin' the world of one more piece of trash!" David Lark toasted the group, lifting his glass.

"Right on!" The usually stolid Hank Pike agreed.

"Looky! Looky!" Jumbo said. "Investigator Gary Keith, here to fill us in on all the grisly details of the autopsy."

The investigator took Midget's usual seat and signaled the waitress. "Scotch. Double. Straight up."

"Hey," Lark said with a nod, "it's the Ice Maiden."

The woman walked by without glancing at them and took a seat at the bar. All the regulars had tried their luck, but the Ice Maiden always left alone. A tall, sleek brunette, the verdict of the officers had been that her buttocks moved in the tight, short skirt like snakes in a burlap bag. The long hair, pulled in a ponytail to one side, added to her aloof appearance. She was about twenty-five.

"That's what I call *class*," Gary Keith whispered.

"Forget it, college boy," Jumbo said, belching. "Everybody who drinks here has tried her out at one time or another. She always leaves alone."

"Maybe they didn't use the right approach," Keith replied, dropping money on the tray of the approaching waitress and picking up his scotch. His eyes were on the woman.

For a half hour or so, Keith hardly took his eyes from her. When other officers discovered he was not in the mood to discuss police business, they ignored him. The subject of .38 caliber versus 9 millimeter versus .45 caliber came up and the discussion was on. After the third scotch, Keith got up and made his way to the bar. The woman gave off a faint odor of honeysuckle as he neared her. His nostrils flared.

"The angels, not half so happy in heaven / Went envying her and me . . .," Gary Keith said, shocked at his boldness. Picking up women in bars was not his style. He felt like a fool.

Then a strange thing happened. She turned slowly, her perfect eyebrows arching and looked him up and down.

"Tell me," she said, "the name of the poem and its author, and I'll let you sit down."

"'Annabel Lee,' Edgar Allan Poe."

"Sit down."

He pulled himself up on the plush leather stool and motioned to the bartender. "What will you have?"

"Rum and cola."

"One rum and cola, one scotch," he told the bartender.

"You were with the cops. Are you a cop?"

"If I say yes, do I have to leave?"

"No. I'm not prejudiced against professions, just ignorance." She finished the rum and cola in front of her and picked up the fresh one as the bartender put it down.

"In that case I *am* a cop, a homicide investigator. What are you, besides one of the most beautiful women I've ever seen?"

"I'm an artist. I do freelance graphics for two or three magazines."

"Art was my minor when I went to UT," he said, sipping the smoky-tasting scotch. "By the way, my name is Gary Keith."

"Tess Pearman," she told him. "Are you married, Gary Keith?"

"Yes, but she's left me with an empty house, and I'm waiting on the papers."

"Doesn't matter. I just wanted to see if you'd be truthful, considering that you're still wearing a ring."

"Yeah." There seemed to be nothing to add that would not sound silly.

"Suppose we go get something to eat, Gary?" She picked up her purse.

"Sure," he said, dropping a bill on the bar. "Don't you want to finish the rest of your drink?"

"No. I want to go somewhere private after we eat, and I don't want my senses dulled. Can you quote the rest of that poem?"

"No, but I have the book at home." He was following her as she made her way through the crowd.

"Looky, looky, looky," Jumbo crowed as Gary and Tess walked by the table. "The college boy has melted the Ice Maiden."

"Well, I say let's drink to Gary Keith," David Lark said. "He's done our profession proud."

"Damn right," Hank Pike agreed.

Linda Keith turned the key quietly, intending to surprise Gary. She had missed him more than she thought was possible. So what if he was obsessed with crime and criminals? It could be worse. Gary was an intelligent, educated man. Some things are more important than money and status.

As she stepped into the empty living room, she heard murmuring from the back. Was he listening to the radio? No, he was crying! She could hear the whimpering clearly.

Poor baby! Her big, strong cop was crying. Tears came to her eyes as she crossed the living room and reached around the bedoom door to switch on the overhead light.

It took her eyes a moment to adjust.

Gary, coupled to a woman with long legs and full breasts, raised up from the sleeping bag on his hands and blinked owlishly. He could not see well without his glasses. The woman, a sleek creature, turned her head and leisurely looked Linda up and down from her position under her partner. She broke the silence.

"Are you a sophisticated woman, or are we going to have a childish scene?"

"Bastard!" Linda spat out, turning to go. "My lawyer will send you the papers." The front door slammed.

"You definitely have good taste in women, Gary Keith," Tess said. "She's beautiful."

"Thanks."

"Would you like to recover before we continue?"

"I think that's a good idea," he laughed. "A very good idea."

137

Chapter Nineteen

Mac Ferguson cursed silently to himself as he got off his John Deere tractor. Six silver garbage bags were piled in the gully, just off the dirt road that divided the two sides of his farm.

Now he knew why the old pickup truck had been prowling around a few nights earlier. Whenever vehicles penetrated so far back from the road, it was either lovers or people dumping garbage. Mac always prosecuted when he caught them, but the old truck had gotten away.

A mongrel dog looked up, then ran with a yelp as the farmer bent over for a rock. People who allowed their dogs to roam free were another of his pet gripes.

What was that smell? Obviously something dead. He stepped down into the ditch to throw the bags out. He would pick them up later. He grabbed the tied top and picked one up. It was heavy. Throwing it out of the ditch, he grabbed the one the dog had been chewing on. It spilled out, dumping decayed flesh and moiling, white maggots on the ground.

He staggered away from the horrible sight and smell, retching. He needed the police, most definitely.

The two stood on the porch as the wrecker backed into the driveway. Larry Foglesong's old Chevrolet was attached to the back of it.

"Whatta ya think's goin' on?" the man asked.

"I don't know," the woman replied.

The wrecker driver got out. An enormously fat man, he was sweating, even though it was a cool day. Taking off his hat, he removed a red and white bandana from his hip pocket and wiped sweat from his forehead. Then, spotting them on the porch, he waddled in their direction.

"Are y'all Eddie Courtney and Alma Thurber?"

"What if we are?" Courtney asked suspiciously.

"Don't give me a hard time," the fat man said, "not if you want me to leave this car."

"Who told ya to leave it?" Alma asked.

"The cops did. The old woman whose son was chopped up went back to Ohio. She left word to bring it out here after the cops got through with it. Are you Courtney and Thurber?"

"Yeah," Eddie said, "but we ain't got no money to pay for a wrecker bill."

"There's no charge," the fat driver said, turning away. "Jeez, I never had so much trouble *givin'* anything away before."

After the wrecker driver unhooked the car, grunting and wheezing, he left. The two of them walked to the car and stood looking at it like two children.

"See," he said, "I told you there wouldn't be no trouble with the car."

"We *did* have a accident," she muttered from between thin lips. "There coulda been problems."

"You never quit, do ya?" he snapped. "This car was never so clean when Larry drove it. *Was* it?"

"No, it was a mess before we cleaned it up. That's the truth."

"Come on," he said, limping to the driver's side and opening the door with his good arm. "Let's go for a ride."

"How many garbage bags do you think we've looked through?" Doyle asked, sipping at a cup of coffee as they bumped down the back country road.

"I don't know, but I'm definitely tired of it. I'll be glad to wrap this one up. That must be our complainant just ahead, there by the green tractor."

"That ain't just a green tractor, Gary. That's a *John Deere*," Doyle corrected him.

"What's the difference?"

"Would you call a Corvette just a car? I can tell you're a city boy."

"And proud of it," Keith replied, pulling in behind the tractor.

A man dressed in bib overalls came toward them as they got out of the unmarked cruiser. He appeared upset.

"I'm Mac Ferguson. I own this place. There's somethin' bad in the ditch. Real bad. I knew the people in that old pickup truck was up to somethin' the other night, but I never expected nothin' like what I found."

"When did you see this old pickup truck, Mr. Ferguson?" Gary Keith asked.

"It was the night before that torso was found. I remember because I'd been plowin' the clover under in that field over yonder." He indicated a northerly direction. "I'm always gettin' kids parkin' and people dumpin' garbage. They got away, though, and this mornin' was the first time I was over here again. It's bad, I'm tellin' ya."

"What exactly do you have, Mr. Ferguson?" Griffin asked.

"Dead meat and maggots. I gotta strong stomach and I nearly puked. If you don't mind, I'll stay over here while you check it out. The smell's real bad."

"Point out the place, Mr. Ferguson," Doyle said.

"It's right over there. Ain't you guys got gas masks or somethin'? I'm tellin' ya, it's disgustin'."

"Nope," Doyle replied, heading in the direction the farmer had pointed. "We just make do with what we have."

When they were within fifty feet of the ditch, the smell assaulted them. Glancing at each other, they both took out handkerchiefs to cover their nostrils.

"Well, it's definitely bigger than a rabbit or a squirrel," Doyle commented.

140

The odor was overpowering at the edge of the ditch. Doyle motioned the younger officer back, then jumped down for a closer look. He peered at the maggots, now scattered over the ground, forcing himself to take in details.

Standing back a few feet, Keith watched Griffin pick up a stick and rip the plastic of another bag, then a third, and a fourth. He wondered if he would ever have the internal discipline required of a homicide investigator.

After a few minutes of probing around in all the bags, the tall, lanky sergeant stood up and jumped lightly from the ditch. The two of them retreated to the road.

Removing the handkerchiefs from their nostrils, they both breathed deeply.

"Is it another body?"

"Not unless it was some kind of mutant," Doyle replied, wiping tears caused by the overpowering odor.

"Say what?" the farmer asked. Keith merely looked puzzled.

"There's nothin' in the bag except ribs."

"Ribs? Who would dump a couple hundred pounds of ribs?"

"A group of outlaw bikers who stole them and ate all they wanted," Doyle explained.

"Yeah," Keith agreed quietly, "the kind of people who don't donate to charity. If you have something and no place to store it, you just drive out in the country and dump it. Especially if you don't want the cops to catch you."

"You two have lost me," the farmer said, shaking his head.

"Sorry, Mr. Ferguson. It's kind of an inside joke about outlaw bikers, motorcycles, and torso killin's."

"Yeah, and it looks like the joke was on Bonzo," Gary snickered.

"Sammy Turpin ain't gonna be too happy either," Doyle reminded him. "He had his heart set on sendin' the whole Devil's Sons club up for murder."

"*Please?* What are you two talkin' about?" the farmer asked.

"Well," Keith replied with a smile, "it all started when our criminal intelligence officer was watching a motorcycle club have a party. They were fixing ribs, but the officer didn't know it . . ."

"Did you call for an officer?" Jumbo asked the fat woman in the polka dot dress.

"Yes, I did," she snapped indignantly, waddling down the rickety wooden steps. "Over an hour ago."

"I'd have been here sooner," the big man replied, "but there were some people hurt in a car wreck. We have to take care of injuries before property crimes." Jumbo worked hard at being polite. He needed no more complaints about his "attitude."

"There's always an excuse," she sniffed. "If this was the west end, you'd have been here sooner, I bet. We never see a cop up here—until *after* somebody steals what we work so hard for."

"Yes, ma'am, it's an unsatisfactory situation, but I have two calls waitin' when I finish here. Could you give me the details please?"

"Follow me, I won't keep you any longer than I have to," she said sarcastically. Jumbo followed, repressing an urge to plant a size-thirteen boot on her yard-wide behind.

"There, the door with the hinges off. He broke into the smokehouse and stole two hams."

"When did you discover the break-in?" Jumbo asked, ready to jot down notes.

"I didn't *discover* it. I heard him break in and saw him leave, carrying two of my best hams!"

"Can you describe him?"

"Of course I can."

"Then *would* you, please?"

"He was big. Not tall, but real broad, with black hair. I only saw him from the back. He was wearin' a lightweight brown jacket, boots, and blue jeans."

Jumbo finished the report, tuning out the fat woman. There were hardly ever any burglaries in the beat he was working. Now there had been two in twenty-four hours.

He shrugged to himself. Maybe crime was infectious and everyone was being affected by the torso found just two miles away.

Chapter Twenty

"Here you go, sailor, have another belt of grog," Tess Pearman teased, handing him a plastic drinking glass half-full of good scotch.

"Are you tryin' to get me drunk, lady?" Gary Keith asked as he took it from her. He was obviously already quite drunk. When drunk, his college diction slipped back to local dialect.

"You obviously needed to get drunk and cry on my shoulder."

"I don't know why," he slurred out the words. "Ever'thing's cool. My wife is divorcin' me, and I just blew my first homicide invest'gation. Ever'thing is comin' up strawberries, or whatever the hell kinda fruit is supposed to come up."

Tess reached for a pack of cigarettes lying by the mattress that had replaced the sleeping bag in Gary's bedroom. Her breasts jiggled slightly as she sat up.

"You have beautiful tits," he said.

"Thanks." She lit the cigarette and inhaled deeply.

"I mean it. You read about perfect, cone-shaped breas', but you've got the firs' pair I've ever seen." He leaned over and rubbed his cheek against the breast nearest him, "They feel cool to the touch . . . like a little puppy dog's nose."

"You're a frustrated poet, Keith. Lay off the nipple, unless you're ready to commence action again."

"You're right." He sat up and slurped the scotch. "I'd probably just fail at that, too."

"Don't you think you're overreacting a little? After all, it was just a lead that didn't work out."

"No, no, no . . . you don't unner'stand. *I* was the one fol-
lowin' the bad lead. I thought the bikers did Foglesong in. Ol'
Doyle Griffin, he thought it was the butcher from the begin-
nin'. He's got the street instincts. All I got is a degree in crimi-
nology."

"Did Griffin say that?"

"Nope. Ole Doyle said not to be discouraged, 'cause you
always go down a lot of dead ends. But *he* didn't. Oh no. *He*
latched right onto it at the first. *Ritualistic,* he said. And he
was right, I bet."

She pushed the dark hair back from his high forehead. "It'll
all look better when you sober up. Besides, you don't know
that Griffin has it solved. He may be wrong too."

"Maybe. Maybe I oughtta go to law school like Linda says."

"That bitch doesn't know what she's talking about! What
kind of intellect sees a pretty face as an accomplishment? Besides, you'd be miserable as a lawyer."

"And her ass ain't half as nice as yours, Tess. Honest Injun,
cross my heart." He spilled more scotch.

"What time are you supposed to go to work?" Tess asked,
stubbing out the cigarette.

"At seven o'clock," he answered. "Pour me another, will
ya?" He extended the tumbler, still half-full.

"Where's your book of phone numbers? It's five o'clock
now. I'm going to call in sick for you. You definitely won't be
in any condition to work today."

"It's in my coat pocket. But if I don't work today, ole Doyle
will have the case solved. He never blows *his* cool." He
watched admiringly as she trotted across the room.

"You've got one fine ass," he mumbled.

"You're right about my ass, but you're wrong about your
partner. Everybody blows their cool sometimes. You just
haven't seen him do it yet."

Doyle pulled up in front of Sarah Trinkle's house.
A small, white clapboard trimmed in red, it reminded him of
a gingerbread house from a children's story.

144

Gary had called in sick, though Doyle suspected he was hung over. The young investigator had been pretty let down to find out that the Devil's Sons had not killed Larry Foglesong. Of course, they had been unable to question any of the club members, but it was fairly obvious what had happened. They *had* stolen the motorcycle, but they had nothing to do with the killing. Bonzo had died because of stolen spareribs.

Keith had a lot to learn about failure.

Doyle had decided to visit the modern-day witch early, halfway hoping to catch John Waters at her house. There would be no report on the blood samples for a few days, but he was sure he could squeeze a confession out of Waters.

The detective was almost certain that Waters had butchered the body, for whatever reason. It was obvious that he was an unstable man. On the other hand, Sarah Trinkle seemed stable and sane, despite her professed belief in witchcraft, or *Wicca* as she called it.

He rapped lightly on the door, then drew a deep breath as she opened it. She stood naked in her pink and blonde glory, all five-feet-eleven of her. Her hair tumbled in waves over her shoulders.

"Come in," she said, "I've been expecting you. You'll have to sit a few minutes, though, I'm working on a spell."

"I can come back," he said through a dry mouth, trying not to stare at her.

"No, that's all right." She stepped aside. "You were expecting John to be here. He isn't, but he did show up the night before last to pick up a brown jacket he'd left."

Doyle hoped his suspect was not in the house. A murder suspect was the last thing on his mind. He was aroused, and his arousal was fueled by knowing that her nudity seemed so natural.

"Sit on the couch," she said, "and watch if you want. But don't talk. It distracts me."

He sat back, feeling a rush of panic. The smell of herbs permeated the air, and the candlelight from the circle on the floor flickered off the occult objects in the room. He realized that most of the outside light was blocked by black draperies.

As she stepped carefully into the circle, he saw for the first time that she was not totally naked. A white garter encircled her left thigh. Bending over at the waist, she picked up a double-edged dagger and turned. With the dagger, she traced over the circle where she had stepped through, as if closing it back. Walking to the other side, she turned to face him and squatted before a censer where incense was slowly burning.

Gary Keith would have been surprised to see his senior partner at that moment. Doyle was breathing hard, his eyes fixed on her. He was aroused like he had not been since he was a boy. Whatever the consequences, whatever her part in this case, he had to have her—and he knew it.

Professional conduct had departed him. He was caught up in an emotional hurricane. For a moment, as he watched her quietly chant from an open book in front of her, he wondered briefly if she had cast a spell on him. He decided he didn't care.

She went on for perhaps ten minutes, quietly chanting esoteric words, then leaned forward, looking directly at him, and blew out the candle. For a moment he couldn't see her, then as his eyes adjusted, the light from a candle on the kitchen counter illuminated her. She was standing directly in front of him.

"Give me your hand."

Without speaking, he extended his right hand. She took it and guided it between her thighs.

"I felt it when you were here the last time," she gasped. "I felt your lust. We're old soul mates, Doyle." Sarah turned and walked to the bed in three strides.

In less time than he thought possible, Doyle was sinking into her with a loud moan. He was lost in her.

Less than three miles away, John Waters sat quietly, munching on a piece of ham. He was considering trying to see Sarah. He was tired of sleeping on the ground, and he was filthy. Besides, he needed to check up on the news. Maybe Sarah's magic had worked by now.

John very much wanted to believe that.

Slicing off another piece of ham, he opened a pack of saltine crackers he had stolen from a small grocery store down the road. Never a thief, he felt vindicated by circumstances. What was he supposed to do?

Where had he gone wrong? How had he drawn the attention of the police? It had to do with his mother, but he wasn't even certain what made her suspicious. After all, he had been at it for over two years.

More than seventy-five times he had sharpened his tools and worked his magic. There was power and satisfaction in the clean slice of a sharp blade. The navy had taught him how, and he had polished his skills.

A carcass seemed to melt under his hands. The smell of blood had never repulsed him as it had others.

It was over now, however. That was for sure. Even if Sarah's magic kept him from prison, he would never again dare to use the workshop.

There would be no more evenings ending in elation, no more of Sarah's overspiced meat pies waiting at the end of a hard day.

He wrapped the ham in a brown bag he had taken from the grocery store and stood, looking out the door of his cave. His father had never found it. No one, not even Sarah, knew it existed.

It was here that he had brought his fantasies to life. Here he had slain his father a thousand times in his dreams. Here he had first used the knife to gut small animals he had killed.

He walked to the mouth of the cave and looked around. About thirty feet in the air, no one could see it without climbing the almost vertical face of the ridge.

Working his way down, over footholds his body knew by memory, he decided to stake out Sarah's house. Moving into the woods, he began to work his way in that direction. The only sound as he silently moved through the trees was the sound of a squirrel chattering.

"What do you want to drink? I have diet soda, tea, and coffee."

"No witches brew?" Doyle asked from the bed. He watched her, still naked as she went through the refrigerator. The hum of the microwave oven and the smell of spices filled the room.

"Fresh out."

"All right, then, coffee will do."

"It should be champagne, Doyle. I'm still tingling down to my toes."

"I bet you say that to all the cops you screw." He lit a cigarette, staring at her through lowered lids.

"Don't joke! And don't tell me you didn't feel it. We merged, Doyle. Our souls intermingled."

"All right. It was the best sex I ever had in my life. I'm glad it was, since it's the most unprofessional thing I've ever done."

"Everyone needs to break the rules some time." Her laughter was distinct, like the tinkling of a bell.

"You don't understand," he said, "I've compromised an investigation."

"No, you haven't." The microwave jangled. She picked up a pot holder and lifted the steaming meat pie out onto the counter. "The investigation will come to nothing. I told you, I raised the cone of power."

"I don't guess you'd want to talk about that little workshop of John's and what he does in there?"

"Of course not. I have principles, too—not to mention client-patient privilege. I wouldn't betray a trust. Besides, I've never been there. Why don't you tell me what you *think* he does?"

"I can't do that."

"Why not?" She spooned the steaming, spicy dish onto two plates and carried one to him.

"Because you're suspect as an accessory."

"Really? Well, the cone will protect me, too, so don't worry. Everything will work out fine."

He shook his head, smiling, and took the plate from her. "Ahh! This smells good. What is it again?"

"It's what most people wouldn't think of eating. It's liver, heart, and sweetbread."

"What's sweetbread?" He plunged his fork in and speared a piece of meat.

"It's the thymus and pancreas. Old-timers called it the neck sweetbread and the stomach sweetbread. It's seldom eaten now," she said.

"Well, I never knew what I was missin' and I'm an old farm boy. Is there some kind of symbolism here?"

"Yes. The heart, liver, and sweetbreads are the seat of the soul. We consume the essence of the creature who gave it up."

"I don't know about *that*," Doyle said, putting the bite in his mouth, "but this has to be the best meat I ever put in my mouth. I've never had anything like it before."

"I can believe that," Sarah said with a smile. "Eat up, there's plenty more where that came from."

Sonofabitch! Bastard! Cocksucker! John Waters cursed to himself as he ran back through the woods. The cop was there again at Sarah's house. It was the same one, the tall, silver-haired one who had violated his workshop.

There would be no hot bath or hot meal for John Waters. Worse, he was running out of food. Tonight would mean another raid on the small grocery store.

"Damn that cop! Damn him!"

Chapter Twenty-one

Doyle was already at his desk, reading the newspaper, when Gary Keith arrived. The ashtray, freshly emptied every morning, was overflowing. Beside the ashtray was the folder on Larry Foglesong's murder.

"You feelin' any better?" Doyle asked, lighting a fresh cigarette.

"I wasn't sick. I was drunk and in bed with this fabulous girl I met the other night."

"Don't let the lieutenant hear you say that. Probably wouldn't be a good idea to let your wife hear it either."

"My wife has left me, Doyle."

"Oh?" Griffin's eyebrows lifted. He put the newspaper on the desk. "Would you like to talk about it? I ain't a psychologist, but I've had two wives."

"Two separate worlds, Doyle. That's the problem. Money and high social standing versus my career." Keith went to the refrigerator and got his usual diet lemon-lime drink.

"Gary, I think you'll find that no matter who you marry there'll be two separate worlds, unless you marry another cop."

"I know. It's probably for the best. How are the papers treating us?"

"Well, we're on page three of the morning paper. They've run another quotation from that psychic Samantha Thorpe. They called her up and she has renewed her offer to help us solve this case. Seems like everyone has already forgot that she predicted another murder for Halloween. They're still callin' it the 'Jigsaw Man case.'"

"I guess people are going to believe what they want," Keith said. "Did you get anything out of the witch yesterday?"

For a moment, Griffin got a faraway look in his eyes, as if startled in a remembrance.

"Yes and no. Waters was there the night after we caught him in his little shop of horrors. He picked up a brown coat he'd left earlier. She hasn't seen him since."

"Have you pointed out that she can be charged with being an accessory after the fact in a first-degree murder case?"

"No. We've got a little game goin'. She acts like she has no idea why we want to talk to Waters, and I've not told her any different. Besides, she claims privilege because she's a licensed therapist."

"I doubt that client-therapist privilege would hold up in a murder case," Keith said. "If you're stringing her along, though, that's good. He could be in Borneo by now. We may end up watching her mail."

"Naw. Waters won't go far. He's a screwed-up mama's boy. He'll surface in the vicinity."

"Let's hope so," Keith replied, sipping his drink.

"I'm countin' on it. What have you got lined up today?"

"I'm going to check burglaries in the area around Waters' house. He has to be eating. Later this evening, I'm going to roll call and alert patrol to be on the watch for him."

"Good idea. I'm gonna spend the day goin' through this case file. Sometimes you miss something you should have seen." Griffin took out the Polaroid picture of Larry Foglesong's head. "Take this picture. There's a message here, but it won't quite come into focus. It will, though. Eventually. And I'll kick myself for not seein' it sooner."

"Delta 7, possible burglary of a business in progress," the dispatcher said. "Mike's Micro-mini Mart on Gilbert Springs Road. Complainant says he heard someone break a window. Be advised there was a burglary there over the weekend."

"10–4," Ruth Ames replied.

"Delta 9," David Lark interjected. "I'll assist Delta 7."

Ruth glanced at her dashboard clock, noting that it was less than twenty-five minutes until shift change. She hoped it was a flight of imagination on the part of the complainant. If she had to write a burglary report, it would push her. The idea that the burglary might still be in progress never crossed her mind. Thieves seldom are caught inside the building they are robbing.

"I'm on the scene," Ruth said. Killing the lights, she got out of the cruiser, a nine cell, cast-aluminum flashlight in her left hand. At the side of the building, she paused. A window was out.

"Delta 7, speed up that other car, I have entry," she spoke into her portable radio.

Watching the window, she edged around to the back of the building. The door was closed, as the front door had been. It was just possible . . .

The back door exploded. Ruth went for her pistol, but the burglar, head down, already had slammed into her midsection with his shoulder, knocking her to the ground.

She rolled over on her stomach and aimed her pistol at his retreating back, gasping for air. She did not pull the trigger, but grabbed her radio again.

"Delta 7 . . . burglary suspect . . . eastbound on Gilbert Springs . . . suspect *was* inside."

"Are you all right, Delta 7?" David Lark asked. "I'm almost there."

"10–4. I'm . . . just winded. He's a *big* sucker, David."

"I see him!" The pitch of Lark's voice went up. "And he's seen me! Get back-up rollin' this way. He's headed across the field toward the dairy farm."

David Lark bailed out of his cruiser and vaulted over the fence. The suspect was about seventy-five yards ahead of him, clearly visible in the bright moonlight. Lark smiled to himself and let his legs stretch. Besides harrassing outlaw bikers and drinking beer at Neptune's Lounge, his only other love was distance running. He had placed in the top five at the Police Olympics two years in a row.

The distance closed quickly. Thirty feet behind the suspect, Lark slowed so as not to overtake him. There was no weapon in sight, but Lark was taking no chances.

"Stop! Police!" he yelled.

The man was big, and he ran clumsily. He suddenly leaned forward, picked up a tree limb, and whirled to face the officer. Alerted by his change in stance, Lark halted twenty-five feet from him. Lark's Glock 9 millimeter semiautomatic pistol was aimed at the man's chest.

"Drop it or die." Lark said.

"Kill me!" the man screamed. "Go ahead. I ain't goin' to jail." He brandished the crooked tree limb.

"You don't want to die," Lark argued. "And I don't want to kill you. Put it down."

Lark heard footsteps approaching. In a moment, Ruth Ames was on the scene, standing off to Lark's right, baton in hand. The suspect, wild-eyed, with dark hair and several day's growth of beard, was focused on Lark and did not appear to have noticed the woman officer.

"Burglary isn't such a big deal. Hardly anybody goes to jail for that. Put the stick down. Do it now!"

"You don't understand," the big man sobbed. "They know all about my workshop. Shoot me! *Do it!*"

Ruth had been edging in. Without warning, she sprinted toward the suspect. He turned, attempting to swing the club, but it was too late. Her hard plastic baton arced down and slammed into his wrist. As he tried to pull away, she drove the end into his midsection.

He collapsed with a grunt and hissing breath.

By the time he caught his breath, the officers had rolled him over and cuffed him. He was crying like a baby.

"Good work, Ruth. I thought I was gonna hafta kill him for a second there."

"Delta 7, to dispatch. Call unit 323. Have them meet us at the jail. I believe we have the suspect they told us about at roll call earlier today."

Gary Keith was talking to Patrol Officer Ruth Ames when Doyle arrived. She was drinking coffee from a plastic cup, nodding. The first officer on the scene when the silver garbage bags had been discovered, she had written a thorough report. Doyle decided to put her in for a commendation and to recommend her for investigator.

She was a pale blonde woman, with hair pulled back in a bun. She lost none of her femininity, though, despite her slightly chunky build.

"Ruth says she thinks Waters is ready to talk," Gary Keith said. "She and David Lark caught him on a grocery store burglary."

"He's been crying and talking about his workshop, Sergeant. Says we know everything now. I think he may be a little claustrophobic," the patrol officer said.

"He probably is. There'll be a letter in your folder for this bust, Ruth. We appreciate it."

"No big deal." She knew she had been dismissed. "Keep me updated," she said, walking away.

"I had him brought up to the interrogation room," Keith said.

"Gary, I'm gonna pull rank on you. You've done a good job, but this interrogation is important—"

"If you think I'm going to miss this interrogation, *Sergeant*—"

"Calm down! It's your case and I want you in there, but I'll ask the questions. We can't be at cross-purposes on this."

"Sorry. I didn't mean to snap at you. I understand. This is your interrogation."

A husky jailer looked them over and unlocked the steel door. Inside, John Waters sat at a table, head in hands. He looked up as they entered and raised his head. For a second there was a flash of fire as he saw Doyle, then it went away.

"John, I'm Sergeant Griffin. This is Investigator Keith. We need to ask you some questions." Keith unobtrusively set a small tape recorder on the table and turned it on.

"I know who you are," Waters said in a flat voice. "My mother called you, and you took my tools. You've been at Sarah's house, too. But Sarah didn't know nothin' about what I was doin'."

"I believe that, John. You want a cigarette?"

"I don't smoke."

"John," Doyle lit a cigarette for himself. "I think you'll feel better after you get everything off your chest, but first we have to read you your rights."

"I'll tell you anything you wanna know. It don't matter. I'm gonna kill myself the first chance I get. I can't stand bein' locked up."

"Now, don't talk like that, John. Listen carefully. You have the right to remain silent. You have the right to the presence of an attorney . . ."

Waters sat quietly. When Griffin was finished with the *Miranda* warning, Gary Keith slid a dated waiver of rights form across the table and handed him a pen.

"If you understand your rights, say yes and sign the form," Doyle told him.

"Yes, I understand." He scratched his name, his hand dwarfing the pen, then gave the form and the pen back to Keith.

"John," Griffin put out his cigarette and reached for another. "How long have you had your workshop?"

"About two years."

"What do you do there?"

"You know what I do."

"Tell me about it."

"I'm a meatcutter. I cut up carcasses."

"Do you work alone, John?"

"I do all the butcherin', but somebody else brings them in. They pay me for the work."

"How many . . . how many times have you worked for these people you're talkin' about, John?"

"Seventy-five times."

Doyle glanced out of the corner of his eye at Keith, fearing he would say something. Seventy-five bodies would make this the biggest confirmed mass murder in police history. Keith was merely sitting with his mouth open, thinking of how he would look on national television.

"Tell me how it works."

"They leave a message on a bulletin board at a laundromat. That's how I know when they're gonna bring me some work. I got in touch with them through a guy I met at a community college. The only one I ever see is the guy who delivers and picks up."

"John, just before Halloween you did some work, didn't you? But you left some bloody clothes and your mother found them. Tell me about that job. Everything you can remember."

"I wondered what got her suspicious." He looked at Doyle, his dark eyes flashing briefly. "My own mother turned me in."

"Tell me about it, John."

"What's to tell? He delivered it. I butchered it and put it in the garbage bags like I always do."

"You put everything in the garbage bags?"

"Yeah. Well, everything except the heart, liver, and sweetbreads. I took them to Sarah. She thinks they're magic and makes meat pies out of 'em. The pies are a little spicy for my taste, but she likes 'em."

Noting the expression that had come over the detective's face, John Waters became alarmed.

"Sarah didn't know nothin' about where I got that stuff. I told her I was butcherin' beef for the neighbors."

Doyle Griffin pushed away from the table. He had gone pale and was swallowing hard. He staggered a step and began to beat on the steel door. When an alarmed jail guard jerked the door open, Doyle shoved by him. He held the nausea down until he got to the restroom. The guard could hear him throwing up.

"Lock the door back," Keith said, "and make sure Sergeant Griffin is all right." Gary did not want to lose momentum.

"John, what do the people you work for do with the . . . meat you cut for them?"

"They sell it to specialty restaurants. There's a big demand for it."

They sat staring at each other in silence. The conversation was becoming more bizarre all the time. Gary was feeling a little nauseous himself.

"They sell it to restaurants?"

"Yeah, the meat goes to restaurants. Stuff like paws and antlers and teeth go to people who ship to the Orient. A bear's gall bladder is worth a couple hundred dollars by itself."

"What the hell are you talking about?"

"Poachers," Waters replied, a puzzled expression on his broad, whiskered face. "I butcher deer and bears and wild hogs killed around here. Most of 'em come from the Smoky Mountains National Park. There was a big bust a few months ago. It's a federal offense, you know." He covered his face with huge hands and began to sob again.

"So when the officers drove in on you the other night—"

"I'd butchered a deer that night. I thought it would be safe that one last time. I didn't get the blood cleaned up, though. So now you've got me. I can't stand being locked up!"

Gary Keith picked up his recorder and turned it off tiredly. He rapped on the door, and the husky guard opened it. "Is Sergeant Griffin still in the restroom?"

"Yeah," the guard replied. "He's quit throwin' up."

A few minutes later, he found Griffin sitting on the floor of the restroom, wiping his face with a wet towel.

"Doyle, I don't know what made you sick, but I'm about to make you feel worse."

"Gary, it's not possible to feel any worse than I do."

"John Waters did not kill Larry Foglesong, or anyone else."

Doyle's head snapped up. "He just confessed."

"No, he just confessed to illegally butchering deer, bears, and wild hogs for a gang of poachers."

157

"And you believe him?" Doyle was hopeful, but not quite ready to accept the news.

"I have to. I just checked the mail. Records put this in our box after we left yesterday afternoon." He extended an envelope. "It's the lab report on the blood samples from John Waters' workshop. The blood wasn't human. It came from a ruminant mammal of the family *Cervidae*."

"Speak English, Gary."

"The blood came from a deer."

Doyle threw back his head and began to laugh. He laughed until tears flowed freely. He laughed until he had nearly lost his breath.

"You're pretty happy for a detective who just lost his last lead on a highly visible murder case. We're back to square one, you know."

"That's all right, Gary." Doyle wiped his eyes with the wet towel. "We'll solve it. Tomorrow we'll start over. We've missed something, but it's gotta be in the file somewhere."

"If you say so."

"Take my word, son. Tell the jail to take our hold off Mr. Waters so he can make bail on the burglary charge. I'm going home and drink some beer."

Gary Keith shook his head as the senior detective walked down the hall, still chuckling to himself.

Chapter Twenty-two

Doyle rolled over and looked at the clock, then sighed deeply. One of those people who is awake for the day when he wakes up, he had slipped into bed at 1:30 that morning. Now he was awake at four o'clock.

He had dreamed of Polaroid pictures of severed heads and of giant black cooking pots around which withered old hags stood cackling as their brew bubbled and boiled. Some of his best hunches came to him as he was waking up or just before he went to sleep.

Sitting up on the bed, he noticed his reflection in the mirror across the room. *Getting old,* he thought. Very few dark hairs still mixed in with the white. He padded into the kitchen and turned on the coffee maker. He always put in the water and ground coffee before going to bed.

In the living room, he lit a cigarette. A few minutes later he was lighting a second as he poured himself a cup of hot, black coffee. He decided to put in a little time at the potter's wheel before his shower.

He had already pulled his stool up before he saw the pink envelope on the center of the wheel. It had his name in black ink, inscribed in Trish's no-nonsense, heavy strokes. She had put it exactly in the right place to make sure he found it. He opened it, fairly certain that it was not an invitation.

Dear Doyle,

I have been offered a job in Atlanta. It will mean a substantial raise in pay. Today I decided to accept it. Of course, I couldn't find you to talk it over. We never have talked, have we?

By the time you read this, I will be on my way. I know you don't like long good-byes, so . . .

Doyle tossed the envelope into the wastebasket and unwrapped a lump of clay from a piece of damp cloth. There had been a lot of good-byes in his life. It would have come sooner or later, and he was relieved, although he would miss her. But for the time being he was relieved he'd only have to report his whereabouts to the dispatcher.

He reached down and switched on the electric wheel. In a moment the room was filled with its familiar hum.

As Doyle was sitting down to the wheel, an amazed John Waters was receiving his property back and signing a bond release. The only charge placed against him was burglary. He was certain that the store owner, a man with whom he had gone to school, would refuse to prosecute if he paid for the damages and the small amount of food he had taken.

What about the illegal butchering of animals? Was Sarah's magic protecting him? he wondered.

"This way, Mr. Waters," the jailer in blue poplin told him. "There's a lady waiting outside."

As the iron door clanged shut behind him, flooding him with relief, Sarah got up from one of the plastic and metal waiting room chairs. She was dressed in a black turtleneck sweater and black slacks. A single silver pentagram hung from her neck.

He went to her, arms extended, but found himself stopping. Her face was as smiling and pleasant as ever, but it was obvious that something was wrong. The intimacy between them had vanished.

"This way, John."

He followed her down the hallway and up the long stairs to the street. Her aging Japanese car was parked near the curb. Inside, she started it and pulled away.

"I was really scared for a while . . . ," he began.

"I told you there was nothing to worry about."

"You don't know what was goin' on. I was involved in a federal—"

"John, I don't *want* to know. The magic worked because basically you're a good person. Mend your ways. Use the power for good purposes."

"Anyway, the jailer told me I could call someone to make bond for me on the burglary charge. I asked him about the other, and he said the sheriff's department doesn't spend a lot of time enforcing federal law. He also said nobody can be convicted of anything without evidence. You know, there's no evidence. I don't even know the people I was working with. All the evidence is gone."

"Everything will be all right, John. Make restitution and stay out of trouble. I told you not to worry."

He turned toward her, staring intently in the light of the dashboard. He was a pathetic sight—dirty with several days' growth of wirelike beard.

"It's over between us, isn't it, Sarah?"

"Yes, John, it is. Every mortal thing comes to an end at some point. Always savor your memories and look ahead."

"Is it because of what I've done?"

"No, John. Not directly."

"Is there another man?"

"Yes, but he doesn't know it yet. He has no idea of the forces at work right now."

"He's a lucky man."

"And you're a lucky man. You have a chance to start over. You need to heal the wounds between you and your mother and forgive her for not being stronger. You need to put your father in the past. He was twisted and sick himself. He's run your life long enough.

161

"Now, I'm going to drop you at your house. Get a hot bath and go to bed. Tomorrow you need to work out your problems with the burglary and start putting your life back together."

"I will," he said in a childlike voice that belied his awesome size.

Gary Keith sat at his desk, sipping his diet drink and flipping through the file for the twentieth time that morning. He had gone home the previous evening, but had found himself unable to sleep. After a few hours, he had returned to the office.

On the desk beside the file folder was a legal pad. On it he had made a list of people to be re-interviewed. The key to unlock the case had to be somewhere in the folder.

A *murder has motive and opportunity,* he reminded himself. With the bikers as suspects, the motive had seemed clear: profit and protection from prosecution.

Doyle had theorized that the murder had been part of an esoteric ritual. The motive, though twisted, would have been clear. Now they had neither motive nor opportunity upon which to build.

So opportunity would have to be the wedge to break the case. Gary had decided somehow to track Larry Foglesong's movements after leaving Eddie Courtney and Alma Thurber. When he got to the end of that trail, he would also find motive.

What could such an apparently harmless individual have gotten himself into that would have provoked such rage? Was it drugs? Gary shook his head at that one. It didn't seem likely.

Somewhere they had missed something. He intended to go back and find out what it was. Someone knew. He thought about starting back at the government-subsidized apartment where Larry had lived. The manager had mentioned a girl with whom the victim had once been involved. Maybe she would be the key.

Looking at his watch, he saw that it was almost seven

o'clock, time to have a leisurely breakfast, then start with the apartment manager.

He jotted a note for Doyle, telling him that he was going to start the interviews over again and that he would be on the air. Maybe Doyle would even remember what it was about the Polaroid that had been eluding him.

Though he would not have admitted it, the fact that Doyle's theory had proved no better than his own had done wonders for Gary's self-confidence. He was still in the ballgame.

He might just crack his first homicide after all.

The man spread the Polaroid pictures in front of him, giggling to himself as he had done a hundred times. The pictures constituted a chronicle of Larry Foglesong's dismemberment, a graphic chronicle that would have made an ordinary person nauseous.

The picture he had sent to the detectives was a part of the chronicle. He had, of course, made sure it was much too blurred for any details of the surroundings to show through.

He giggled again, thinking of how the detectives must have spent their time trying to figure out why they had received the picture. None of their scientific methods would work. He had left no prints and no evidence of the dismemberment.

He was smarter than the cops. He had committed the perfect crime.

"Yeah," he said with a chuckle, "old Larry's gone and he ain't comin' back. Not ever."

Chapter Twenty-three

Gary Keith pulled up in front of the ramshackle house that had been Larry Foglesong's last known residence. He noted with relief that the victim's old Chevrolet was parked in the driveway. At least Courtney and Thurber were home.

His trip to Hartford Towers, the subsidized-housing project, had been frustrating and unproductive. The cynical manager he had interviewed had been fired, her replacement told him. Worse, she had deliberately wrecked the files before leaving. The folder on Larry Foglesong was missing.

The investigator had tried unsuccessfully to interview several elderly tenants, but they spoke only in the most general terms. One of them had mistaken him for an investigator from the Department of Housing and Urban Development. Keith was delayed for fifteen minutes, listening to a barrage of complaints concerning the plight of the elderly.

A kitchen curtain moved as Gary walked up the creaking steps. His knock went unanswered for several minutes. Finally, he pounded with the side of his fist as he yelled out, "Police! I know you're in there, so open the door. Now!"

A crack appeared, and Alma Thurber stared around the door at him.

"I need to ask you and Eddie some questions, Alma. Let me in."

"The wrecker driver left that car. We never went and got it. If they said we did, they're lyin'," she said in a trembling voice.

"Why the hell are you so obsessed with that car? I don't give a damn about the car. I'm trying to find out who killed Larry Foglesong. Now let me in. I'm not in the mood for games."

Reluctantly, she stepped aside. Eddie Courtney sat on the couch, a cup of coffee in his good hand, staring angrily at the investigator.

"You can't talk to us like that just because we're poor and crippled," Courtney complained. "We got rights, too."

"Yes, you do. But you also have obligations. One of those obligations is to cooperate in a murder investigation."

"We done answered your questions," the man replied.

"And you'll have to answer them again."

"All right, but I don't like it. I'm gonna call your boss and say you was rude. You're only doin' us this way because we can't afford a fancy lawyer."

"That's fine," Gary said, "just as long as you answer the questions."

Alma Thurber sat, her strong right hand clasped in the partially paralyzed left one. Her body was tense, but her face was emotionless. Keith wondered how much was attributable to her stroke and how much to personality.

"Alma, tell me how you first met Larry Foglesong."

"It was when he started botherin' her at the TV room at Hartford Towers—" Courtney began.

"I'm talking to Alma," Keith interrupted. "Let her answer the questions. I'll get to you."

"Well, he asked me out the first night he was there—"

"But she turned him down," Courtney began. "She never went out with him!"

"Courtney, I said let Alma answer her own questions!" The man sat back, lips compressed, dark eyes flashing.

"Well, Alma?"

"I never really went out with him—like Eddie said—but he'd come to my room sometimes. That was why him and Eddie started arguin'. Eddie didn't want him around unless we was all three there—"

"He said indecent things! That's why I wanted to be there. He tried to get Alma to—"

"Courtney, if you butt in again, I'll take you downtown and question you separately! Now be quiet.

"Alma, you and Larry were closer than you let on before, weren't you?"

"Well, I guess so . . ." Her eyes were downcast.

Courtney suddenly stood up, startling Keith. He moved in his shuffling walk toward the kitchen.

"Don't leave, Courtney. I need to ask you some questions, too."

"I'm just goin' to get some more coffee. You want some?"

"No, thanks." Keith stared at him for a moment. He didn't think the man could move very fast if he did try to walk out.

"Tell me how close you and Larry were, Alma. It's all right. I need to know everything I can about Larry so I can track down whoever killed him."

"When Larry first moved in, he'd play cards with me and Eddie. Then one day while Eddie was gone, he come to my room and we . . . you know . . . did it."

Suddenly Keith remembered the earlier conversation about how Courtney was impotent and how angry the man had been about the revelation. The truth of what had been going on dawned on him, just as Alma's eyes darted to a point above his head, then quickly away.

Motive *and* opportunity! It had been there all along! They had overlooked it because of the seeming helplessness of Foglesong's roommates. Gary willed his legs to move, but it was too late.

"Old Larry's gone and he ain't comin' back—not ever!"

Keith heard the words as he was trying to move, just before the lead pipe in Eddie Courtney's good right hand made contact with his skull. There was a kaleidoscope of colors. Then everything went black.

Doyle took the Polaroid of Larry Foglesong's severed head down the hall to the photo lab. Sergeant Wick, the technician, was sitting at his desk, feet propped up, reading a *Penthouse* magazine.

"What can you tell me about this picture?" Griffin asked, tossing it on the desk.

Wick, a chubby man of forty or so who managed to look sloppy even in a tuxedo, picked it up and examined it.

"It's a Polaroid of a severed head, or maybe a Halloween mask. It's badly out of focus because the lens was too close to the object. It's sitting on some kind of yellow surface, and there's a disgusting pink wall behind it."

"I know that. Can we trace the film? Can we enhance the picture?"

"Hell, Doyle, I'm just a photographer. I guess maybe the film's numbered. I never had any reason to ask. There's no way to enhance the picture, not that I know of."

"I saw this movie," Doyle said, "where they took a Polaroid negative and got a picture off of it with some kind of computer program."

"I saw the movie, Doyle. I guess maybe if you had the resources of Naval Intelligence or the C.I.A. you might work somethin' up. But, hey, look around. What you see is what I've got."

"Thanks, Wick." Doyle took the photo and went back to his office. Picking up the lukewarm coffee, he lit another cigarette.

That certainly didn't help much, he thought as he took a mouthful of coffee. He already knew it was a severed head on a yellow surface with a pink background. Doyle paused, coffee cup in midair.

He grabbed the telephone and dialed dispatch. "This is Sergeant Griffin in homicide. See if you can raise Unit 323, Gary Keith, on the radio." He waited impatiently for the dispatcher to return.

"Sergeant, Keith reported that he was in service at seven this morning, but he doesn't answer. I've tried him on all channels."

"Thanks." Griffin hung up the phone.

The piece had dropped into place. He knew what had been eluding him about the Polaroid. It was Gary's case, though. Doyle did not want to steal his thunder.

Most likely, Gary had gone to breakfast and had forgotten to turn on his radio. It happened all the time. The note he had left said that he was going to start interviewing the same witnesses again.

Maybe he had turned the radio down so as not to disturb anyone. The squawking made some witnesses extremely nervous. On the other hand . . .

Griffin got up quickly. He gulped the last of the coffee before grabbing a fresh pack of cigarettes from the desk drawer. Pride or no pride, he needed to talk to the young investigator before he got in over his head without knowing it.

It was easy to do. After all, he had twenty years of experience himself, and he had overlooked the obvious.

How could anyone blame him, though?

Chapter Twenty-four

Gary Keith's head was throbbing on the right side. He didn't know what Courtney had hit him with, but it had done the job.

He tried to move his wrists, but without success. Opening his eyes, he saw he was tied with nylon cord, wrapped like a mummy, sitting up in a chair.

"You needn't try to get up. Eddie put your handcuffs on you before he tied you up."

Alma Thurber was sitting directly in his line of vision. Her weak hand was clasped in the good one, and on a table beside her was a cup of coffee. Her expression was flat and disinterested.

Gary moved his head. For a moment he thought he would throw up from the knifelike pain.

"Where's Eddie?"

"Gone shoppin'."

"Why did Eddie kill Larry Foglesong, Alma?"

"'Cause Larry could do it so good and Eddie couldn't do it at all. First Eddie liked to watch. Then one day Larry laughed at him. That was before we moved from the apartment."

"Alma, the sheriff's department knows where I am. You can't get away with hurting me. Why don't you cut me loose. You're not in a lot of trouble now, but Eddie is. If anything happens to me, they'll throw the book at you, too."

"We watched you through the window. You didn't talk on the radio before you got out."

With a stab of terror, he realized that she was right. He had violated a fundamental rule: keep the dispatcher notified of your whereabouts at all times.

"Alma, a police car sticks out like a sore thumb. You can't get away with this."

"Eddie says we can. He says he committed the perfect murder already." She took a sip of coffee.

"If it was a perfect murder, I wouldn't be here now, Alma. Just cut me loose, and you'll be all right. I'll see to that."

"Eddie's done hid your car in the garage. Tonight he'll take it and leave it somewhere."

"Alma, *I* found out. Other investigators will, too. You kill a cop, and they'll never rest until they get you."

"You never woulda found out if it wasn't for me. I can't lie good. Eddie knows that. He hit you in the head because he knew I'd let somethin' slip. We're movin' to my sister's place in Ohio after Eddie—"

"Alma! It won't work!"

"Eddie says it will. If we had buried the head instead of throwin' it off the bridge, you still wouldn't know who the body belonged to."

"Yes, we would. There was a tag on the suitcase. We raised Larry's name off of that."

"Well, Eddie says he won't make no mistakes this time." She took another sip of coffee.

"How long will Eddie be gone?"

"Not long. He went to buy some more tools. We throwed the other set away."

A chill seized Gary Keith.

"I know, Alma," he said with inspiration born of desperation. He searched his memory. "Eddie used a hacksaw, wirecutters, an ice pick, and a fish fillet knife. He wore brown cloth gloves. You put them in a paper bag and threw them under the Turner Street viaduct. Right?"

"Yeah, but there ain't no prints because Eddie wore gloves."

Keith knew he had to get loose before Courtney returned. Griffin would eventually track him here, but he did not want to be a jigsaw puzzle when his partner found him. Maybe, just maybe, he could bring some remorse to the surface.

"Alma, tell me all about what happened. I'm not going to be able to tell anybody. I'd like to die knowing the truth."

"I guess it don't matter," she said, getting up and shuffling to the kitchen for more coffee.

"Me and Eddie moved out here after they threw us out of the apartments," she said, taking her seat again. "There ain't no bus out here and cabs is expensive. When Larry showed up, Eddie decided to get him to move out here so we could use his car and get part of his check."

"How did you talk him into it, Alma?"

She sipped the coffee again before answering. "We had this camera we bought at a flea market. You know, the kind that makes pictures right then. Eddie made some pictures of me nekkid. The next time Larry come over, Eddie let Larry look at 'em.

"Larry got all excited. He was always quick to get excited. Eddie said he wanted to make some pictures of Larry . . . you know, doin' it to me."

"Was Larry a good lover, Alma?" Keith asked quietly, hoping to stir a tender memory.

"Oh, yeah, he was good. It lasted a long time, usually."

"So what happened to change things?"

"Well, Larry was a big eater. Groceries was costin' a lot more. He didn't wanna go out in the car much, either. The thing that really got Eddie upset, though, was Larry makin' fun of him.

"Eddie liked to watch at first. Then Larry started sayin' stuff like, 'Don't you just wish you had one that worked?' Eddie got so mad one day that he tried to start a fight. Larry just laughed and smacked him in the face.

"Next day, Eddie said he was gonna kill Larry. While we was shoppin' a few days later, Eddie sneaked and bought the tools and gloves."

"Why did you go along, Alma? You're a decent woman." Keith would have laughed at his own hypocrisy had he not been so terrified. The woman stared at him, her pale watery eyes still without emotion, her wispy brown hair falling across her forehead limply.

"Larry wasn't always that nice to me, either. He talked about how much younger and prettier the biker women was. He said he'd take them over me any day. He said doin' it to me was like stickin' it in the Grand Canyon. Besides, he was spendin' most of his check on that motorcycle and on them whores. Eddie said if we killed him, his checks would keep on comin' and we could cash 'em and nobody would ever know."

"So Eddie decided to do it, and you were afraid to say no?" Keith asked, trying to steer her away from responsibility. She went on in her toneless voice as if he had not spoken.

"Eddie had bought some more film, too. He told Larry he wanted some pictures of us doin' it. That was fine with Larry. We went in the bedroom. I got on top of him. Eddie went around like he was gonna shoot pictures from behind Larry. Then he hit him in the side of the head with the same pipe he used on you."

Keith listened in horror, mesmerized by the unfeeling tone of her voice. She could have been reciting the plot of a soap opera. His mouth had gone dry. He desperately pulled at the cuffs, but they were latched tight.

"Larry was still breathin', so Eddie stabbed him in the eye with the ice pick. When he pushed it in, Larry started thrashin' around. Eddie twisted and pushed it, but he kept movin'. Eddie screamed then. He said, 'Die you sonofabitch, die!'

"Larry finally stopped movin', but he was still breathin'. Eddie went and got a plastic bag and put it over his face. After a while, he died."

"Then what?" Keith asked in morbid fascination.

"Eddie brung in this big piece of plywood. We rolled Larry off on it and drug it to the kitchen. It was hard. When we got him in there, Eddie had me fix some coffee.

"We drunk the coffee and Eddie told me we'd have to cut

the body up in pieces on account of we're both handicapped, you know.

"We had to wait at least a day. Eddie said it wouldn't be so messy then. We had to walk around him here in the kitchen, but Eddie was right. Hardly any mess got off the board and on the floor when Eddie cut him up."

She finished the coffee and went to the kitchen to make more.

Keith sat, trying not to hyperventilate. A sheen of sweat had appeared on his lip. More horrible than the scene she was describing was the calm manner in which she was talking.

He pulled desperately at the cuffs. He had to get loose before Courtney returned.

It was then that the door opened. Gary's heart began to pound harder, and his breath felt like fire in his lungs. It was too late.

"I see the cop's awake," Eddie said, limping into the kitchen. "I brung some presents for him.

"Did ya hear me? I got ya some things, Mr. High and Mighty Cop!" Eddie Courtney leaned forward, almost nose to nose with the investigator. His face was a mask of twisted glee. "Wanna see what I've brung you?"

"Eddie," Keith swallowed hard, "things are bad enough now. If you kill me, they'll track you down. I'm telling you—"

"You ain't tellin' me nothin'!" Courtney screamed. He slapped Keith across the cheek with his good right arm, bringing tears to the investigator's eyes.

"People like you been tellin' me things for years. Now *you* can listen. Understand?"

Keith nodded his head.

"He's been listenin'," Alma said. "He wanted to know everything that happened that day. I got to the part about draggin' Larry to the kitchen," she said in her monotone voice.

"I'm glad he's interested, 'cause I'm gonna show him some pictures. But first I want him to see what I brung 'im."

Courtney held up a shopping bag. Smiling, he took out an

ice pick and held it up. "Look, Mr. Cop. This is to drive into your brain. You won't thrash like Larry did, on account of you're tied tight.

"And here's the knife I'll gut you with and the hacksaw and the wire cutters for the joints and the bones. Ain't you got somethin' to say now, Mr. High and Mighty?"

Keith shook his head. He was concentrating on breathing properly. He did not want to disgrace himself. He had made a serious error and was about to pay for it with his life. He had always hoped to die with dignity. He wondered if he would scream involuntarily when the ice pick went in.

"Go get the pictures, Alma. I want him to see what I'm gettin' ready to do to him."

She went wordlessly from the room. Courtney shuffled to the stove and Gary could hear him pouring fresh coffee. His own tongue was dry. He almost asked for a drink of water, but decided against it. It would only give Eddie Courtney something else to gloat about.

Alma returned with a manila envelope. Courtney shuffled over, coffee cup in his good hand and stood by Keith.

"Show him the one of you first," Courtney said, drinking his coffee. A trickle of it ran down from the side of his mouth.

Alma held up the Polaroid in front of his face. Her features were devoid of expression. In the picture, she sat naked on a chair, legs spread. Her eyes were closed and her mouth was opened.

"Take a good look, Mr. Cop. It's the last one you'll ever see. Show him the next one. Old Larry's gone and he won't be back again—not ever. He won't need that donkey dick of his." Courtney giggled.

"Go on, show him some more. I got pictures of *everything*. And you got one, don't you, Mr. High and Mighty? I sent it to you. I took that picture while old Larry's head was settin' on that counter over there."

It was a nightmare from which he could not wake. Gary sat, unable to move as Alma put each grisly picture in front of him. He thought it would never end. It was almost a relief when Courtney stopped her. He knew what was coming next.

"Take off your clothes, Alma. I want it just like the last time." Courtney was breathing hard. "Let him see you nek-kid!"

She quickly unbuttoned her faded blouse. As it came off, revealing sagging, leathery breasts, her face became mobile for the first time. Her eyes had life in them. She leaned against the couch clumsily, slipping out of her trousers, then limped into Keith's line of sight. She was breathing hard now.

Gary saw Eddie Courtney's evil smile. Slowly he raised the ice pick, lining it up with the officer's right eye, inches away. Keith drew a deep breath, preparing himself.

"Good-bye, Mr. High and Mighty."

Courtney jerked back as the sound of breaking glass and splintering wood from the flimsy door filled the room.

"Back up!" Doyle Griffin yelled. "Move back or I'll kill you."

"No!" Courtney screamed in outrage. His prize was about to be denied him. Desperately he raised the ice pick high for a hard downward thrust.

The room was suddenly filled with the sound of gunfire and the acrid smell of gunsmoke. Keith did not count the shots, though he would later learn that Doyle had fired three times. He only knew that the ice pick had not descended.

Staggering backwards, Courtney clutched at his chest with his one good hand, then fell, a bloody froth on his lips. Alma stood quietly, looking down at him. Once more her face was expressionless.

"It don't matter," Courtney said with a bubbling sound, looking up defiantly at Keith. "Old Larry's gone and he ain't comin' back . . ." His head dropped to the floor, and he did not move again.

Doyle Griffin came across the room, two-inch revolver pointed at Courtney. He watched him for movement, then breathed a deep sigh.

"Partner," Gary Keith said in a hoarse, dry voice, "you came through like a movie cop on this one. I'll never complain about you checking behind me again."

Doyle took out a pocket knife and began to cut the nylon rope away.

"The truth is, Gary, I wasn't checkin' up on you. You owe your life to the interior decorator who painted this humble little abode. I finally realized what was botherin' me about that Polaroid picture."

"What are you talking about, Doyle?"

"The color scheme. That counter over there, where Courtney took the picture of Foglesong's head. It's yellow floral. He blurred the picture enough to obscure the pattern, but nothin' could hide that horrible flamingo pink wall. A while ago, I remembered where I saw that color combination. It was right here when we questioned Alma and Eddie before."

"Thank God for bad interior design," Gary Keith said.

Chapter Twenty-five

Samantha Thorpe was readying herself for the afternoon press conference. She piled on the make-up base, thinking how much more it took every time to cover the wrinkles at the corner of her eyes. She also was developing a permanent crick in her neck from holding her chin high enough to prevent the sag.

It had even occurred to her of late that she might want to change her hair to a more current style.

She was in Horton to drum up a little publicity and sell some books. A mainline bookstore (as opposed to an occult bookstore) had actually taken a hundred of them on consignment. Samantha would be on hand to sign books and arrange consultations of a psychic nature.

It had required quick work. She had begun her calls within minutes of hearing that there had been arrests in the Jigsaw Man case. She had made arrangements for books to be shipped and for a press conference with two local television stations, as well as the Horton papers.

Samantha was an old hand on matters of publicity. On a slow news day, and she was hoping it would be a slow day, she could get almost anything on television as desperate producers tried to fill empty air time.

Besides, there was always interest in things occult. Some were believers, others merely curious. Samantha earned her living from curiosity and gullibility.

She knew it was irrelevant that her predictions had been nowhere near the truth. She had prophesied that the killer would be "sophisticated, highly intelligent . . . an artist, perhaps . . ." So what? Samantha knew perfectly well that most people would "remember" only what she told them she had said.

If anyone actually brought clippings with exact quotations, she would merely drop dark hints that the two deluded people in custody had merely been pawns of a dark and diabolical genius.

It would be a no-lose situation. She would sell books and pick up psychic consultations, no matter what happened. Like a traveling medicine show, Samantha could take advantage of any crowd that gathered.

The phone jangled, and she laid aside her make-up brush with a frown. Who would be calling? She hardly knew anyone in this town. "Hello?"

"Beware the package," a female voice said at the other end.

"I beg your pardon?"

"Beware the package." The phone went dead.

"How strange," she said to herself. "What package?"

In a moment she was engrossed in her make-up. It had probably been a mix-up. She had just finished one eyebrow, heavily done, when there was a knock on the door.

Irritated, she got up and opened it a crack. A young man in a grey uniform stood on the other side.

"Messenger service," he said. "I have a package for Ms. Thorpe."

"I didn't order anything."

"The card just says 'To Samantha, world's greatest psychic.' We had instructions to deliver it at exactly three this afternoon."

The inscription won her over. She opened the door and took the package. It was small, about the size of a shoe box. Halfway across the room, she remembered the phone call with a pang of alarm.

Slowly she lifted it to her ear. There was a definite ticking sound. Samantha put it down gingerly on the bed and backed to the door. In a moment she was running down the stairs, not waiting for an elevator.

She burst into the lobby of the hotel, out of breath, long blue-black hair flying and with only one eyebrow penciled on. "A package . . ." she gasped, ". . . my room . . . 305 . . . telephone call . . . ticking . . . call police!"

The frightened desk clerk was dialing the emergency number before she finished talking.

"Ladies and gentlemen," the Channel 12 field news reporter said, "we are coming live from the scene across the street from the downtown Clairview Hotel, where a drama has unfolded.

"Within moments we should be hearing from a special police bomb squad, which has gone inside to check a mysterious package delivered to Samantha Thorpe, a visiting psychic from South Carolina. Ms. Thorpe is waiting with us.

"Could you bring us up to date, Samantha?"

"Yes, John, I'll be glad to." Samantha's face flashed across Horton. In her frightened rush from the room and the events that followed, she had forgotten that only one of her eyebrows had been penciled on. For her it seemed a windfall of publicity. None of the male television crewmen had been inclined to tell Samantha how silly she looked with only one eyebrow visible.

"Less than an hour ago, I received a telephone call from a woman who told me to 'beware of the package.' Minutes later, I received a ticking package, about the size of a shoe box. I very calmly walked to the front desk and reported it."

"The officers are coming out!" the reporter announced, abandoning Samantha momentarily. "They are carrying the package. Apparently, if it was a bomb, it has been disabled."

"Lieutenant," the reporter yelled at the approaching officer, who was removing his protective mask. "What did you find?"

The lieutenant, a large beaming, Nordic type with pale eyebrows and hair, waited for the cameras to focus in on him.

"What we found was an alarm clock. Also, inside was a note written on paper scented with some kind of herbal odor. It says," he held it up and read, "'If you were a real psychic, you would have known this was just an alarm clock.' The note was not signed."

It was a policeman who first giggled, but it spread quickly through the crowd. Samantha was trying to push through and get inside the building, but the newsman pursued her.

"Samantha, Samantha, what do you have to say about this?" He pushed the microphone under her nose.

"I think . . . I have been treated atrociously—and I don't think the police should read my mail."

Somehow the single eyebrow detracted from her righteous indignation.

It was a bad day for Samantha. She canceled her appearances and news conferences and went back to South Carolina, vowing never to return to Horton.

Doyle Griffin wiped tears from his eyes. He could not stop laughing for an hour after the six o'clock news ended. Later he remembered the bomb squad officer's comment about the "herbally scented note."

"Naw," he finally said to himself, and started laughing again.

Epilogue

"I see the usual crowd is in place," Gary Keith murmured as he and Tess entered Neptune's Lounge. They were both dressed for an evening of celebration, beginning with drinks, then dinner and dancing. Doyle Griffin had even put aside his dislike for cop bars and was meeting them with his date. The officers looked in their direction as they crossed the floor to an empty table. Keith could not hear what was being said, but he could guess.

"Looky, looky, looky," Jumbo crowed to his companions. "Gary Keith is with the Ice Maiden. That boy definitely has somethin' that we don't know about."

"A toast," Midget Poplin said, "to Gary and the Ice Maiden."

"To Gary and the Ice Maiden," David Lark and Hank Pike joined in.

"Well, would you look at that! Sergeant Doyle Griffin has just honored the lounge with his presence tonight," Jumbo exclaimed.

"Look at his date," Midget said in awe. "She looks like a Viking woman."

"We got to transfer over to homicide division if that's the kind of women they attract," Jumbo announced.

"I'll drink to that," Hank Pike agreed.

At the table, Gary Keith stood gallantly as Doyle pulled out a chair for his date.

"Hello," Tess extended her hand to Doyle's companion. "You must be Sarah Trinkle. I'm Tess Pearman. Gary tells me you're a witch."

"Yes, I am." Sarah smiled.

"It must be fascinating work."

"You meet a lot of interesting people," Sarah agreed, glancing at Doyle with a smile.

Gary Keith sat beaming with pleasure. He knew Linda would have been drawn up in a tight knot, coldly looking down her nose at Sarah and Doyle.

Ahh! It's a good day to be alive, he thought.

Across the room, Midget, Jumbo, and the others had begun toasting the letters of the alphabet. They had reached the letter D by the time the couples left for dinner.